DOCTOR WHO

HEART OF STONE

Trevor Baxendale

The Doctor, Amy and Rory are surprised to discover lumps of moon rock scattered around a farm. But things get even stranger when they find out where the moon rock is coming from – a Rock Man is turning everything he touches to stone! Can the Doctor, Amy and Rory find out what the creature wants before it's too late?

Also available:

The Good the Bad and the Alien
by Colin Brake

System Wipe by Oli Smith

Coming soon:

Rain of Terror by Mike Tucker

Extra Time by Richard Dungworth

The Underwater War by Richard Dinnick

Terminal of Despair by Steve Lyons

DOCTOR ᴅⱳ WHO

HEART OF STONE

Trevor Baxendale

Cover illustrated by Paul Campbell

Want to get closer to the Doctor
and learn more about the very best
Doctor Who books out there?

Go to
www.doctorwhochildrensbooks.co.uk

for news, reviews, competitions

and more!

CONTENTS

PROLOGUE
NIGHT TERRORS

Ralph Conway woke up in the middle of the night. He could hear dogs barking outside.

Ralph climbed out of bed with a groan. He wasn't so young anymore, and he was stiff as a board.

The dogs were barking furiously now.

Ralph looked out of the window, but it was difficult to see anything in the dark. Something was driving those dogs wild, though.

'Four o'clock in the morning!' Ralph grumbled, as he pulled a coat on over his pyjamas.

He went downstairs and switched on the kitchen light. He hoped it would scare off any intruders. Then he pulled on a pair of boots and unlocked the back door. He paused to pick up a torch and a heavy walking stick. Anyone caught lurking outside would get a whack with that stick!

It was a chilly, moonlit night. The dogs had stopped barking now, which Ralph thought was strange. The sudden silence was frightening.

Ralph walked slowly across the yard. The dogs were hanging back, whining, almost as if they were scared. That didn't make Ralph feel any better. He had lived on the farm all his life and he knew the area well – it was isolated and exposed.

Suddenly there was a terrific noise – a great, splintering crash in the night, like a juggernaut plowing through a wall at top speed.

The dogs ran yelping back to the farmhouse. Ralph, his heart pounding, shone his torch into the darkness. The wall at the end of the yard was completely destroyed – there was rubble everywhere. Something huge and heavy had smashed clean through.

Ralph moved cautiously forward, stick raised. He would defend himself if he had to.

But no matter where Ralph shone his torch, he saw nothing other than shadows. Apart from the damaged wall, there was nothing to see. There were lumps of stone strewn all around the yard, though, where the wall had been hit.

Through the break in the wall, Ralph could see a car in the distance. The glow of its headlights moved along the main road on the far side of the valley. It was too far away for him to hear it, but it made him think. It was possible, Ralph thought, that a lorry could have crashed into the wall. The bend in the road going past the farm was a well-known accident black spot. A reckless driver could easily lose control of his vehicle.

But where was it now? There was no sign of any car or lorry at all. And Ralph hadn't even heard an engine.

But there was *something*.

The noise of stone moving across stone – a dull, heavy scrape.

Ralph swung his torchlight around the yard, but there was nothing to see. The barn, the tractor, a rusty old plough. Clumps of straw and mud and some puddles reflecting the light of the moon.

Scrape, scrape . . .

There *was* something there, Ralph was sure of

it. Something moving in the shadows. He aimed the torch again, and this time his hand was trembling. The light flickered across a coil of hosepipe; the water trough; a collection of tools leaning against the outhouse . . .

And then he saw it.

Something huge – lumbering – walking on two legs like some kind of giant . . .

And then it was gone, disappearing into the shadows again.

Ralph's heart hammered in his chest and his mouth went dry. He shone the torch around the yard, but there was no sign of the strange figure.

Whatever it was . . . had gone.

Ralph licked his lips. Perhaps it had just been his imagination. That was the only explanation, surely. He was still half asleep. His mind was playing tricks on him.

The dogs were whimpering again. Ralph peered down at the rocks strewn across the yard.

They shone like bone in the cold moonlight and Ralph shivered . . .

CHAPTER 1
CONWAY FARM

The TARDIS appeared in the middle of a pigsty. Startled, the pigs ran around in panic, snorting and squealing and slipping in the wet straw.

Eventually the harsh wheezing of its engines diminished and the TARDIS stood, proud and blue, next to the water trough.

The Doctor stepped out of the TARDIS and immediately greeted the pigs. 'Good morning!'

But the pigs had already decided to ignore the box and anyone who emerged from inside it. As long as they were fed and watered, they didn't really mind who shared their sty.

The Doctor looked like a tall young man with a shock of untidy dark hair and mischievous, deep-set eyes. He wore a tweed jacket and bow tie, with narrow trousers tucked into old boots. He smiled at the pigs as they snuffled around in the straw. 'Lovely morning!'

'Pigs!' said Amy Pond, as she followed the Doctor out of the TARDIS. She wrinkled her nose. 'Phew…'

'*That* is the scent of the countryside,' said Rory Williams, as he stepped out into the ordure covering the ground. 'Yuck.'

Amy and Rory were the Doctor's current travelling companions. She was young, pretty, with striking red hair and trendy clothes. He was tall, rather awkward and dressed in jeans and a warm padded jacket.

Not in the least bit put off by the pigs, the Doctor locked the TARDIS, clearly intending to stay. 'Just what we need,' he told his friends. 'A nice breath of fresh country air.'

'Fresh?' Amy repeated doubtfully.

'Hey!' a voice called out. 'You can't leave that thing in there like that!'

They all turned to see a young woman striding

towards the pigsty in mud-splattered wellies and a thick, padded coat. She had dark hair tied back and a seriously cross look on her face.

The three travellers turned as one to look at the TARDIS. The space and time machine was disguised as an old police box and so it looked decidedly out of place in the pigsty. But then, the TARDIS looked a bit out of place *anywhere*.

'You'll frighten Old Percy,' the young woman told them. 'She's pregnant, y'know!'

'Percy?' said Rory with a frown.

'Pregnant?' said Amy.

'Long story,' sighed the woman. 'Look, you can't stay in there. You'll have to leave the box where it is, I suppose.'

The Doctor, Amy and Rory climbed over the low fence surrounding the pen and introduced themselves.

'My name's Jess,' the woman said. 'I've come to feed Old Percy. She needs twice as much as normal – she's eating for six at least.'

Jess heaved a bucket of slops into the trough

and the pigs got stuck in, heads down and ears flopping. The yard was quickly filled with the sound of chomping and snorting.

'How on Earth did you get that thing in there anyway?' Jess asked, nodding at the TARDIS.

'Well, it just sort of materialised there,' replied the Doctor.

Jess raised an eyebrow. 'Oh, it did, did it?'

'Ask Old Percy.'

Jess patted the sow's back. 'She's a bit busy now,' she said with a smile. 'I'll ask her later.'

'Do you work here, then?' Amy asked.

'Of course. This is Conway Farm. It may not look like much, but I call it home.'

The little farm overlooked a wide valley. The sky above was full of clouds and the promise of rain. A sharp breeze carried the smell of grass and soil and animals across the fields, and Amy shivered in her short skirt. She wasn't dressed for farming.

'Let's get you in for a cup of tea,' laughed Jess. 'We don't often get visitors here!'

They followed Jess along a narrow, rutted track

until they reached the farmhouse. A burly man with a hard, grizzled face was busy repairing a broken wall. He wore thick gloves to protect his hands and an old flat cap.

Rory whistled when he saw the full extent of the damage. There was rubble and bits of broken brick scattered everywhere. 'What happened here?' he asked.

'Somethin' costin' me time an' money,' growled the man. He didn't sound at all happy.

'This is my dad, Ralph Conway,' said Jess. She introduced the Doctor, Amy and Rory.

'How do,' grunted Ralph, touching his cap before returning to his work.

'There was an accident here last night,' explained Jess. 'Smashed the wall to bits. Dad's got to fix it.'

'An accident?' repeated the Doctor. He was looking at the smashed stones all over the yard.

'We think a lorry or something must have crashed into it last night,' Jess continued. 'Plenty of trucks miss the bend in the road and skid if they're not careful.'

The Doctor looked at the road and nodded thoughtfully. 'Yes, I see. Or rather, I don't.'

'I beg your pardon?' Jess said.

'No skid marks,' said the Doctor. 'Nothing to show any kind of vehicle coming off the road.'

'Uh oh,' said Rory quietly to Amy. 'He's getting all curious . . .'

Amy smiled. 'Probably thinks it was hit by a meteorite or something.'

The Doctor had picked up a piece of stone from the ground. It was a pale grey colour, roughly the size of a tennis ball. He weighed it in his hand and sniffed it. Then he looked around. There were plenty of stones like this littered across the yard.

'All this damage,' said the Doctor. 'And no sign of a lorry or a car, or anything.'

Ralph was watching the Doctor carefully. It was clear that he was interested in what the Doctor had to say. He straightened up and said, 'Well, what do you think did it? Cos I can't work it out!'

The Doctor was smiling. 'I've really no idea,' he said. 'But I'd love to find out!'

'Are you from the insurance company?' asked Jess, as if suddenly struck by a thought. 'Come to assess the damage?'

'No, I'm just a nosy parker,' the Doctor replied. 'For instance, this stone interests me enormously.' He held up the fragment of grey rock between his finger and thumb for all to see. 'This isn't local stone, is it?'

'No,' answered Ralph. 'There's loads of it around this morning, though. I thought it might have fallen off the back of the lorry.'

'The lorry that doesn't actually exist,' pointed out Amy.

Ralph shrugged. 'I dunno. But it isn't stone from around here – that much I do know. I thought maybe it had come from Derbyshire.'

'It's from considerably further away than Derbyshire, Mr Conway,' said the Doctor. He held the stone up towards the sky. 'This piece of rock has come all the way from the moon!'

CHAPTER 2
A HOLE IN THE WALL

The Doctor was sitting at the kitchen table, examining the lump of grey rock with his sonic screwdriver.

Amy and Rory were holding mugs of hot tea, while Jess opened a packet of chocolate biscuits and put them on the table.

'Got any Jammie Dodgers?' asked the Doctor without looking up. 'Always liked a Jammie Dodger.'

'Sorry, just these,' smiled Jess.

'These are fine,' said Rory, delving into the packet.

'You'd best take them away,' Amy told Jess, 'before the Cookie Monster here eats them all.'

The Doctor looked up sharply. 'Did someone say monster?'

'Not that kind of monster, silly,' laughed Amy.

'Anyway – it's breakfast,' Rory protested, munching on another biscuit.

'Breakfast?' queried Jess. She was peering into the oven, where a large pot was simmering. 'It's nearly time for dinner.'

'It's hard to keep track of time where we come from,' explained Amy. 'That smells good, though. What's cooking?'

'Lamb stew,' smiled Jess. 'Don't worry, there's enough for everyone.'

'Oh, no, we're not staying –' Amy said, but the Doctor interrupted her with a loud exclamation.

'Look at this!' The Doctor shut down his sonic screwdriver with a satisfied click. 'Definitely moon rock,' he announced. 'High concentrations of anorthite, pyroxene, mare basalts and titanium. And lots of armalcolite – a new and unique mineral named after the crew of Apollo 11: *Arm*strong, *Al*drin and *Col*lins. So – without a doubt, moon rock.'

'But how can that be?' asked Rory, reaching for another chocolate digestive. 'I mean, all the way here from the moon. . . ?'

'Did it come down in a meteorite or something?' wondered Amy.

'Meteorite?' queried Jess.

'Yeah, you know . . .' said the Doctor, sitting back and folding his arms. His gaze never left the moon rock, however. 'Lumps of iron, rock, bits and pieces and what-have-you, flying through space and falling into Earth's gravitational pull.'

'So you mean it could be a chunk of the moon that's actually fallen to Earth?'

The Doctor pursed his lips. 'Doubt it. Most meteors burn up in Earth's atmosphere. Very few reach the ground – and if they do, then they're big enough to cause a heck of a lot of damage.'

'There *is* a lot of damage,' Jess pointed out.

The Doctor was still staring at the rock. 'If a meteorite this big had survived the trip through the atmosphere and landed in your front yard, then the whole farm would have been flattened.'

'Oh. I see.'

'There has to be another explanation.'

'Such as?' asked Amy.

The Doctor didn't reply. Instead, he simply picked up the moon rock and dashed out of the kitchen.

When the others caught up, he was standing in the middle of the yard holding his sonic screwdriver aloft. The tip glowed green as he waved it about.

'What is that thing?' wondered Jess.

'Sonic screwdriver,' explained Rory, trying to sound like an expert. 'But it does a lot more than just . . . driving screws.'

The Doctor wheeled around the yard with the sonic, pausing occasionally to check the readings. Eventually he shoved it back into his jacket pocket and harrumphed. 'No sign of any alien spacecraft technology, teleport beam or quantum link. It's a complete mystery.' He sounded insulted, as if nothing had any right to be a complete mystery to him.

'Well something must have brought it here,' insisted Amy.

The Doctor tossed the moon rock from hand to hand, wondering. Then he wandered over to where

Ralph Conway was still working on the wall. 'How's it going, Mr Conway?'

Ralph straightened up, wincing slightly and holding his back. 'Just about done,' he rumbled. 'It'll have to do for now, at least.'

The Doctor surveyed the repair work. You could see quite easily where the moon rocks had been used to fill in the hole, but it was a remarkably good job, nonetheless. 'You've had to use a lot of moon stone,' the Doctor observed. 'And yet it all seems to fit together quite nicely.'

'Well, that's the strangest thing,' agreed Ralph. 'I've no idea what happened to the rest of the wall, but those rocks you say come from the moon seemed to do the trick all right. It's a case of having to make do and mend, Doctor.'

'You've missed a bit,' noted Rory, joining them. He pointed to a hole the size of his fist on the top edge of the wall.

'No, he hasn't,' said the Doctor. He darted forward and placed the moon rock he still had in his hand in the space. It fitted perfectly.

'Well, I'll be . . .' Ralph Conway took off his cap and scratched his head.

'That was lucky,' laughed Rory.

'Nothing to do with luck, Rory.' The Doctor was pacing up and down the wall, rubbing his fingers together as he inspected the wall. 'Dry stone wall, remember. Every piece has a place. These moon rocks are all the exact size and shape necessary to repair the wall.'

Rory frowned. 'But that's impossible – isn't it?'

The Doctor looked up at him, his eyes gleaming. 'No more impossible than finding chunks of the moon on this farm in the first place.'

CHAPTER 3

THE FIRST VISITOR

The Doctor was examining the area all around the wall, front and back, when a sleek red sports car pulled in through the gates and stopped in the middle of the yard with a cheery growl of its exhaust.

Jess walked over to the car, a look of pure delight on her face.

The driver climbed nimbly out of the car, equally happy. He was tall, smooth-faced and good-looking. He wore wire-framed glasses and was dressed in clean corduroy trousers and a fashionable sports jacket. 'Hi there, sweetheart,' he said, embracing Jess warmly.

'Who's the lucky fella?' asked Amy.

Jess led the man over. 'This is Chris,' she said, introducing Amy and Rory. 'My fiancé.'

'Hey — Amy and I were engaged once,' said Rory with a smile. 'We're married now, though. Mr and Mrs Pond!'

'Great to meet you,' said Chris, shaking hands. 'I hope I'm not intruding on anything?'

'No, we're just passing through,' Amy assured him.

'But they're staying for dinner with us,' Jess said. 'I insist. There's plenty for everyone!'

Chris was still smiling broadly, but Amy thought she could detect a slight frown above his eyes. It was almost as if there was something on his mind that he wanted to tell Jess, but would have to keep to himself for now.

'That's great,' Chris was saying. 'The more the merrier.'

'Dinner will be ready in about twenty minutes,' Jess told them. 'Time for Dad to get cleaned up at least.'

Ralph Conway was standing by the wall with the Doctor. They were both examining a rock in minute detail, the Doctor's fingers wiggling over it as he talked about the geology of the moon. When he heard Jess call him, Ralph looked up. He nodded at Chris, but there was no smile. Chris waved back and then followed Jess into the farmhouse with Rory and Amy.

'Trouble?' wondered the Doctor. He had noticed the way Ralph's lips had tightened in disapproval when his daughter's fiancé had arrived.

'Who knows?' Ralph replied.

The Doctor shrugged. 'None of my business, but I can't help noticing that you don't seem too happy to see that young lad.'

Ralph raised an eyebrow, amused by the Doctor's description of Chris as a young lad. The Doctor didn't look any older than Chris himself. 'You're right . . .' Ralph grumbled. 'It isn't any of your business.'

'But you don't approve of him?'

'Jess is my only daughter. I don't want her hurt.'

'You think that might happen?'

Ralph sighed heavily. 'Chris Jenkins is not from around here, Doctor. He's all right in himself – but he's not a country man, if you know what I mean.'

'Ah,' said the Doctor. 'A townie?'

'He doesn't understand farming. And that's all Jess has ever known.'

'She's young. She'll learn.'

'That's what worries me.'

CHAPTER 4
DINNER TIME

Dinner was a lively affair, with an excellent lamb stew served with new potatoes garnished with mint. Everyone agreed that Jess had done an excellent job. Even Ralph Conway looked content. If he disapproved of Jess's boyfriend, then he made every effort not to show it during the meal.

They talked about the weather and the farm and Percy the pregnant pig. But the conversation turned eventually, and naturally, to the disturbance of the previous night, the broken wall and, of course, the strange appearance of the moon rocks.

Chris Jenkins was doubtful. 'Moon rock? I mean, *really*?'

'That's what the Doctor says,' Amy replied, sipping her coffee. She held the mug cupped in both hands for warmth. Rory's arm was around her shoulder.

Chris looked at the Doctor. 'Are you qualified to make that pronouncement?'

'Oh, yes,' the Doctor said. 'Extremely very qualified. And the sonic screwdriver never lies.'

'But the whole idea is absurd,' Chris insisted.

'Are *you* qualified to make that pronouncement?'

'As a matter of fact, I am,' Chris replied evenly. 'I'm a research technician at Henson Labs. I specialise in geochemistry and I've made quite a study of moon rock.'

'You never told me that,' said Jess.

Chris shrugged. 'You know I don't like to talk about my work too much. But the *Apollo* space missions brought back over 380kg of rock samples from the moon landings in the 1970s.'

'Wow,' said Rory. 'And you've seen them?'

'We were lent some samples once. I had to make a study of the cosmic ray and radiation history of the mineral content.' Chris's face broke into a smile. 'It was pretty boring, to be honest. But I have actually handled moon rock, and not many people can say that.'

'That's true,' said the Doctor.

'We could only touch them using gloves and special tools, though,' Chris continued. 'And the security was amazing. Did you know that moon rock is one of the most valuable substances on the planet?'

'Because it's so rare, I expect,' said Jess.

'Not so rare anymore,' said Amy drily.

'NASA still holds most of the samples,' Chris said. 'But many pieces were given away as presents by the US government to foreign countries. Moon rock is rarer than diamonds. Sometimes pieces are sold illegally on the black market at hugely inflated prices – but more often than not they're fakes.'

'How long ago was this?' asked the Doctor. 'When you worked on the moon samples, I mean.'

'Erm – a few years ago. We're currently studying the effects of UV light on lava and ash samples from the Eyjafjallajökull volcano in Iceland.'

'You should check some of the moon samples

we have here,' suggested Rory. 'Could be useful.'

Chris shook his head. 'I don't think so. For one thing, I can't give permission to use the lab facilities. And anyway, I doubt very much that it *is* actual moon rock out there.'

'Well, it is,' the Doctor said.

Chris shook his head, clearly reaching the conclusion that the Doctor was talking rubbish. 'It's nonsense, really.'

'Is it possible there could be a mistake?' wondered Jess, trying to balance both sides of the argument. 'You've got to admit, Doctor, that there's no logical reason why there would be lumps of the moon scattered around our farm.'

'I'd like to run some more tests on the rocks,' the Doctor admitted. 'I might know more then.'

'Sorry I can't help,' said Chris. 'I mean, even if I was allowed, I couldn't do it. We're mad busy at the lab with the volcanic ash. Worked off our feet.'

'Not hard work, though, is it?' said Ralph Conway. He had been quiet for most of the meal, preferring to concentrate on eating instead of talking. He had been brought up in a strict family, where no one was even allowed to speak during meal times.

'Oh, dad . . .' Jess started. 'Just because it's not farm work . . .'

'No, it's OK,' said Chris. 'I understand. I don't do much physical work in my job. It's all up here.' He tapped his forehead. 'But I do keep myself fit. I go to the gym three times a week.'

'Hmm,' said Ralph, wiping his lips on a napkin. He clearly wasn't impressed. He got up from the table and excused himself, preferring not to go to bed too late. 'Farm chores start early,' he grumbled.

'Do you think there might be any more disturbances during the night?' asked Jess. 'Meteorites or crashing lorries or whatever?'

'I doubt it!' laughed Chris.

The Doctor stood up and looked directly at Chris. 'I'm positively counting on it.'

CHAPTER 5
THE UNINVITED GUEST

The Doctor stepped outside and drew a deep breath. It was cold and dark. He looked up at the night sky, searching out familiar stars and constellations through the gaps in the clouds.

It always paid to check that everything was as it should be.

The moon glowed softly.

The Doctor frowned slightly. How could bits of the moon suddenly end up all the way down here, on Earth? And how could they match the size and shape of the stones in Ralph Conway's wall? And why was Chris Jenkins so touchy about the whole subject of moon rock?

The Doctor's lips twitched into a smile. He loved a good mystery.

He retrieved the stone from the wall where he had placed it earlier and set off towards the TARDIS. He had instruments on-board that could tell him a lot more about the origin and structure of the moon rock in his hand.

As he walked up the hill towards the pigsty, a dark cloud drifted across the face of the moon and plunged the farm into an eerie darkness. It may only have been the Doctor's imagination, but it seemed to grow suddenly colder.

And there was a strange feeling in the air, a kind of tension, like the calm just before a storm broke.

The TARDIS windows were shining brightly in the darkness, and the Doctor hurried on.

In the farmhouse kitchen, Amy was helping Jess clear the dirty plates from the table, while Rory and Chris loaded them into the dishwasher.

'So, how did you two meet?' Rory asked. He liked Chris. He seemed decent, if a little overconfident, but Rory didn't mind that.

'Market day,' Chris replied. He smiled at Jess.

'Our eyes met across a herd of cows, and it was love at first sight.'

'Yeah, right,' said Jess ruefully. She scraped some leftovers into a recycling bucket. The pigs would get that later. 'As I remember, Chris stood in a fresh cow pat and blamed me for it.'

Amy laughed. 'Blamed you?'

'It came from one of her cows,' argued Chris.

Jess sighed. It was clearly a well-worn story. 'He was in a suit, with brand-new shoes. I helped clean him up. Things just went on from there.'

'So, I suppose I've got plenty to thank the silly cow for,' Chris said, and they both laughed.

With the dishwasher fully loaded, Jess made a fresh lot of coffee and asked Rory how he had met Amy.

'Oh, we knew each other from when we were kids,' he said, slightly embarrassed.

'Oh!' Jess seemed delighted. 'Childhood sweethearts. And what about the Doctor? Where does he fit in?'

'Erm, the same, really. Amy's known him since

she was seven. Sort of.'

'Oh . . .' Jess looked a little confused. 'Well, he's quite a character. Odd, but in a nice way.'

'I'll be sure to tell him that,' promised Amy with a smile. She picked up her jacket. 'I'm going up to the TARDIS to see how he's getting on.'

Rory made to follow, but she shook her head. 'No, you stay here. Enjoy your coffee. Back soon. See ya!'

Amy shivered as she stepped outside. It was cosy and warm in the farmhouse, but out here it was certainly getting chilly.

She folded her arms tightly and hurried across the yard, heading for the TARDIS. She could see the roof lamp and windows from here, shining out through the night. The sight always gave her a tingle of excitement.

She wondered what the Doctor was up to. She could just imagine him tinkering with the TARDIS control console, fussing around it from panel to panel, checking read-outs and gauges, utterly engrossed in some kind of scientific experiment.

Well, enough of all that, thought Amy. The Doctor could come back and spend some time with ordinary folk, enjoy a cup of coffee, proper conversation. Worry about the moon rocks in the morning.

Amy stepped past the water trough and headed up the slope – just as something huge and powerful suddenly rose up in front of her, right out of the darkness. It filled her vision like a wall of grey stone.

Amy opened her mouth to cry out, but it was too late. The great lump of rock bore down on her like a hammer on an anvil.

CHAPTER 6
ROCK MONSTER

Amy was paralysed with fear for a second. The huge grey figure loomed over her like a statue – but a statue that could *move*. It was easily two-and-a-half metres tall, and looked as if it had been hewn from a solid lump of granite.

The creature reached towards her and–

The Doctor grabbed Amy and hauled her quickly out of the way.

The rock creature made an angry noise that sounded like a pile of house bricks being dragged across concrete. It turned, slowly but heavily, a pair of dark holes in its lumpy face serving as eyes.

Its hollow stare centred on its prey and it growled again.

'What is it?' Amy gasped.

'No idea,' replied the Doctor. 'Saw it on the TARDIS monitor. Look out!'

The creature lashed out heavily. One rock-like fist crashed into a water trough, denting the steel and sending a spray of icy water into the night.

The Doctor and Amy backed away, heading for the farmhouse, just as Jess and Rory came out of it, eyes widening in horror as they saw the creature.

Chris appeared in the kitchen window, a look of shock and terror on his face. In less than a second, he had turned and run into the next room.

'Back inside!' ordered the Doctor, rushing straight past Jess and Rory.

Amy followed the Doctor, yelling, 'Right behind you!'

Rory was about to turn and pelt after them, but a scream from Jess made him pause. The rock monster swung a massive arm, missing Jess by centimetres, but caving in the side of the Land Rover parked outside the house. The door buckled and glass exploded across the yard.

Rory picked up a spare shovel, checked its

weight in his hands, and then swung it like a cricket bat at the monster. The shovel connected with a resounding *clang!* and Rory felt the vibration running up his arms and into his shoulders like an electric shock.

The rock monster turned its attention from Jess to Rory with a gravelly snarl. Rory stared up at the creature. The shovel, which was still quivering like a tuning fork in his numbed fingers, slipped from his grasp.

The monster advanced slowly and purposefully towards Rory.

And then Jess was pulling him back into the farmhouse and slamming the door behind them. She scrabbled for the bolts at the top and bottom.

'That won't stop it,' said the Doctor.

And even as he spoke, the kitchen door shuddered with the impact of a giant stone fist.

'Quick, barricade it!' said Amy, trying to push the heavy kitchen table across the door. The others joined in, heaving the table into place, the coffee mugs rolling around and smashing on the floor.

But the creature wouldn't be put off so easily.

A second fist burst through the remains of the door. The big table skidded backwards, flung aside like an old cardboard box.

A third and final assault on the door reduced it to matchwood.

CHAPTER 7
RUN OR FIGHT?

Shards of wood hurtled around the kitchen as the rock monster smashed its way in. The table was crushed, dashed aside, and then the whole room seemed to shake as the creature forced its way inside. The door frame tore loose from the surrounding brickwork, caught on the stone giant's bulky shoulders.

Ralph Conway's dogs were going berserk. Neither could understand what was happening, but both knew an intruder when they saw one. They snapped and barked and bared their fangs, jumping up at the creature as it seemed to fill the room.

The terrible racket had already brought Ralph running downstairs. 'What in the blue blazes is going on?' he thundered.

But Ralph could immediately see the danger his dogs were in. They could bark as much as they liked, but the thing that had forced its way into his house was just too powerful.

So Ralph grabbed both dogs by the collar and hauled them out of the kitchen, still yelping and barking.

The Doctor and Rory were trying to slow the monster down, throwing kitchen chairs, pots and pans and anything else they could lay their hands on at it. They finally gave up when an orange, hurled in desperation by Rory, bounced harmlessly off the creature's head.

'An orange?' the Doctor spluttered at Rory.

'Nothing left to chuck,' said Rory hopelessly.

'Time to go,' the Doctor said. They backed out of the kitchen, into the narrow passageway that connected the back of the house to the front. The rock monster growled menacingly, crunching its way across the stone floor of the kitchen in pursuit.

Ralph was struggling with the dogs. One broke

free, snapping its jaws at anything that moved. It dived past the Doctor, heading for the kitchen. Ralph lunged after it, yelling for it to come back.

But it was too late. The dog snarled at the rock monster, but one savage swipe of its arm sent the hound spinning across the room.

'Get back!' shouted the Doctor, grabbing Ralph by the arm. But the farmer tore free, cursing the monster with every breath.

Then the creature reached out, grasped Ralph Conway in one giant, crag-like hand and hurled him backwards.

Ralph landed heavily in the passageway, completely stunned. The Doctor and Rory dragged him into the front room, where Jess and Amy were waiting with Chris Jenkins.

Chris had been cowering in the front room ever since he had seen the creature through the kitchen window. His face was white with fear, but he knew he had to do something now. But he couldn't think what.

'Close the door!' screamed Jess.

Chris jumped up and slammed the door shut – but it was a useless gesture. Within seconds, the entire wall was disintegrating in a cloud of plaster dust as the rock creature forced its way through.

'It's unstoppable,' gasped Chris. He sounded utterly panic-stricken.

The rock creature stepped into the front room with a slow, ominous scraping sound. It surveyed the five people carefully, its blank eye sockets full of darkness.

'What is it, Doctor?' asked Rory fearfully.

'More importantly – what does it *want*?' wondered the Doctor.

'What does that matter?' asked Chris. He ran from one side of the room to another in panic. 'It's going to kill us all if we don't do something fast!'

'I'm open to suggestions,' said the Doctor.

'Well, here's mine,' replied Chris. 'Run for it!'

And then he kicked open the farmhouse door and sprinted out into the night.

'Oh, charming!' Amy called after him.

Jess darted towards the door, shouting after Chris, 'Come back! I can't leave Dad like this!'

But it was no use. Chris was gone.

Rory was helping Ralph Conway into an old armchair. The farmer winced as he sat down, one arm hanging limply. A gash on his forehead oozed blood.

But Rory was a trained nurse and knew what to look for. There didn't seem to be any serious damage, but you could never be totally sure with head injuries.

'He's in shock,' he said, peering into Ralph's eyes. They were heavy and a bit dazed. 'I think his arm could be broken too.'

Jess bit her lip, looking from her dad in the chair to the open door. She was torn between running after Chris and staying with her dad.

But there was never really any contest.

She joined Rory by her father's side as the rock monster tore its way through the room. Its hollow eyes scanned the room, searching for its prey.

CHAPTER 8
THE MOON'S COLD GAZE

The monster rose up to its full height with a loud, scraping roar.

Amy turned to the Doctor. 'Do something!'

But the Doctor's eyes were shining. 'No need,' he said.

'What?' said Amy, and she was joined in her gasp of disbelief by Rory and Jess.

The Doctor simply folded his arms and leant against a bookcase.

And did precisely nothing.

The rock monster stomped straight past him and smashed its way through the exit, taking a large part of the wall with it. It crunched its way out into the night and disappeared into the darkness.

'What's going on?' asked Amy, staring out

through the ragged hole in the wall where the door had once been. 'Where's it going?'

'I'd say it was following Chris,' replied the Doctor. He peered out into the night. 'Wouldn't you?'

Everything had fallen unnaturally quiet. The monster was gone. All that was left was a trail of destruction through the farmhouse, bits and pieces of broken masonry and a lot of dust.

'It doesn't make sense,' said Amy. 'Why would the monster be following Chris?'

'*Following* Chris?' repeated Jess.

'Interesting, isn't it?' mused the Doctor.

'Interesting? It's madness!' Jess raised her voice. She stood up from where she had been kneeling by her father. 'I mean, it's just ridiculous. Why would it be following Chris?'

'That I do not know,' said the Doctor. He frowned thoughtfully. 'Yet.'

A lump of brick fell from the lintel over the doorway. Jess slumped in defeat. 'I just don't understand what's happening,' she moaned. 'What on Earth was that horrible thing?'

'That's what I intend to find out,' said the Doctor. He turned towards the wreckage of the doorway. 'Come on, Pond!'

Amy followed the Doctor out into the night, but he had already doubled back to speak to Rory.

'Stay here and look after Mr Conway and Jess,' he said.

Rory looked uncertain. 'What about the rock man? What if he comes back?'

'I doubt that'll happen. He's more interested in Chris Jenkins by the looks of it.'

'But –'

The Doctor sighed. 'Just sit tight here and look after Jess and her dad. They need you.'

'And you don't?'

'Yes – but I need you *here*.'

'Oh. Right. Well, OK.' Rory nodded. 'I'll stay here then.'

'Good man.'

The Doctor turned to leave once more, but Jess stopped him. 'Doctor – I need to know. Will Chris be all right?'

'We'll see,' the Doctor replied, as he slipped out into the darkness.

Chris was still running through the night. At first he had no idea where he was running to – he just had to get away. He had to get away from the insanity of the rock creature, from the Doctor and his friends, from the farmhouse and from Jess.

Occasionally he glanced behind him. He could see the lights of the farmhouse, now in the distance. Above the dark buildings the moon shone brightly. The sight of it chilled him to the bone and made the breath catch in his throat.

Because, no matter how far he ran, Chris knew he would never escape the moon's cold gaze.

Behind Chris, unseen in the darkness, the rock creature trudged relentlessly across the moor.

CHAPTER 9
FOLLOW THE ROCK

The Doctor could move very quickly when he had to – one of the advantages of having a relatively young body. He seemed to run in a tangle of arms and legs, but he picked his way through the trees at quite a pace regardless.

Amy struggled to keep up.

'Hang on!' she called.

The farmhouse was backed by trees, dark and twisted in the night, almost impenetrable. Amy couldn't understand how the Doctor could follow anything through a forest at night.

'How do you know where we're going? I can't even see that rock monster thingy!'

The Doctor hopped nimbly over a fallen tree trunk and skidded to a halt. He was bouncing on his feet, eager to continue with the chase. 'We don't need to see him, Amy,' he said. 'We just follow the trail.'

'What trail?'

The Doctor pointed to the tree trunk. It looked like a thick, pale grey log in the moonlight.

But, as Amy watched, it started to grow paler by the second.

Eventually, with the softest crunch, it turned almost white. It looked as though it had been carved out of solid rock.

Moon rock.

'I don't believe it,' breathed Amy.

'Isn't it amazing?' The Doctor sounded delighted. 'The tree has turned to stone. Lunar stone.'

'But how?'

'Molecular reconfiguration. The creature touched the tree trunk and triggered the change. It did the same thing when it broke through Ralph Conway's wall last night – those stones weren't originally moon rock; they were *changed* into moon rock.'

Amy tried to make sense of it. 'You mean whatever that thing touches turns to moon rock?'

'Pretty much, yeah.'

'Why?'

'I've no idea. Maybe we could ask it – if we can catch it.'

They started off again, and now Amy could see patches of white on the ground every so often, and the occasional stone tree or low-hanging branch perfectly reflecting the moonlight. These were the footsteps – or handprints – of the monster.

'Should be easy enough to track,' she admitted. But she hoped the monster didn't run too far – it was hard trying to keep up with the Doctor as he side-stepped and bounded his way out of the woods.

Before long they reached open ground – moor land. Mist covered the landscape like a thin, silvery sheet. It looked cold and unearthly – like the moon itself. Amy shivered.

The Doctor stopped and whipped out his sonic screwdriver. Its tip clicked open and glowed green as he used it to scan the area. After a few seconds he snapped it shut with a grunt of annoyance.

'It's gone!'

'Gone?'

The Doctor was clearly frustrated. 'Creature, trail, Chris – all gone. No trace of any molecular reconfiguration. It's just disappeared.'

'So what's happened? Has Chris been taken – abducted?'

The Doctor was down on his haunches now, scanning the ground with the sonic. 'It's a possibility,' he replied.

'Oh, no,' said Amy suddenly. 'I've just thought of another possibility.'

'What?'

'Anything the monster touches turns to stone, right?'

The Doctor stood up and frowned at her. 'Yes, right. What of it?'

'It touched Ralph Conway.'

CHAPTER 10
CHANGING

Rory pulled back the curtain and looked out of the window.

The farmyard was moonlit and eerie – everything was a pale grey colour and wreathed in a thin mist. The dented Land Rover looked like a bone-white sculpture.

He could see the front door from this angle, if he craned his neck a bit. The door was gone, smashed into pieces, and the frame was splintered. But it was all shining white in the darkness, as if it was carved out of a piece of the moon.

He let the curtain drop back and turned to look at Jess. 'How is he?'

Jess was sitting on the floor by her father. He was in the armchair growing paler and greyer by the minute. 'I think he's asleep,' she said quietly, 'or maybe in a coma. I just can't tell.'

She was shivering. It was cold in the farmhouse now, with the doors bashed in front and back. Rory thought he could detect the first few tendrils of mist drifting in from outside. He took off his jacket and draped it over Jess's shoulders.

Ralph Conway was still breathing – just. It was shallow, barely visible, but he was definitely alive. Rory wasn't sure how much longer he would last, though. The ugly scar on his forehead looked raw. The rock monster had hit him hard.

'I don't even know if he can see me,' Jess said, waving a hand in front of Ralph's eyes. He continued to stare straight ahead.

'Probably concussion,' said Rory.

'Dad?' said Jess. 'Dad. Can you hear me?' There was no response. She turned to Rory. 'Shouldn't we call an ambulance or something?'

'Er, yes. Good idea.' Rory thought for a moment. 'Take a while to get here though. We're in the middle of nowhere.'

Jess nodded. 'We're a good hour's drive from the nearest hospital. But we could save some time if we drive him ourselves. Use the Land Rover.'

'That could be difficult. The monster totalled it.'

'What about Chris's car?'

Rory bit his lip. He was thinking about explaining all of this to a tired medical doctor in casualty. He really didn't fancy the idea. 'Perhaps we're being a bit hasty, Jess . . . '

Jess gave a hiss of exasperation and turned back to her father. 'Dad! Wake up! It's me – Jess! Come on!' She turned back to Rory once more. 'Where's the Doctor? We need him here! He shouldn't have run off like that!'

'He's not that kind of doctor,' Rory said.

'Then what kind is he?'

'A sort of . . . outer space kind.'

'Don't be stupid,' Jess said angrily.

Rory could tell that she was frightened. And he knew how that felt. 'You saw that rock creature,' he said gently. 'You've seen the moon stones. Trust me, the Doctor will be able to sort it —'

But Jess was no longer listening. She had been distracted by something on her father's face. 'Rory – look!'

Ralph had suddenly turned very pale – almost white – as if the colour had been completely drained from his face. The skin looked dry and dusty.

'Oh, my goodness,' groaned Jess.

Rory peered closer. Then he swallowed. Ralph's eyes were open but grey and opaque.

Something was going horribly wrong.

Rory reached out to touch Ralph's hand. 'Mr Conway . . . ?'

'Don't touch him!' commanded the Doctor, striding into the room with Amy.

Rory jumped back as if stung and Jess gasped with relief. 'Doctor! Thank goodness – what's happening? Where's Chris?'

'He's gone,' the Doctor replied. He tried to make it sound as if this was perfectly OK, but his hands were clenched into fists. 'I'm sorry.'

'Gone?' Jess echoed. Her face had fallen.

'Where?'

'We don't know yet,' Amy said. 'We lost him in the fog. And the monster.'

'And that,' said the Doctor gravely, 'looks to be the least of our problems . . . '

He was staring hard at Ralph Conway, who sat stiffly in his chair, as grey and lifeless as a stone statue.

CHAPTER 11
A NICE CUP OF TEA

The Doctor scanned Ralph with the sonic screwdriver. The green glow passed over the stony features and shone deep into the sightless eyes. Eventually the whirring of the screwdriver ceased and the Doctor flicked it open to inspect the readings.

'Well?' asked Jess. Amy could see that she was worried sick. 'What's happened to him?'

There was a deep frown of concern on the Doctor's face. 'Your dad's been turned to stone,' he said simply. 'Moon stone, to be precise.'

'But how?'

'The rock creature touched him, triggering a complete molecular transformation . . .'

'I mean, how is that even *possible*?'

The Doctor looked closely at Jess. 'Anything's possible,' he told her gently. 'Anything. Including getting him changed back again to the way he was. The way he should be. From what I can tell, the transformation is highly unstable. It could be reversed.'

Jess squeezed the tears from her eyes. 'I hope you know what you're doing, Doctor.'

'Of course I do.' The Doctor turned back to look at Ralph Conway. Unseen by Jess, the Doctor flashed a desperate look at Rory and Amy.

Rory cleared his throat. 'I'll make us all a cup of tea.'

'Yes!' the Doctor agreed. 'Perfect! Just what we all need. A nice cup of tea. Always helps me think . . .' He began to pace around the wreckage of the living room.

Amy was picking up some of the fallen chairs and ornaments. There was moon rock and dust everywhere, but she thought that it probably looked worse than it was. When everything was tidied up, they'd have a clearer idea of just how bad the damage to the farmhouse was.

The Doctor was thinking aloud. 'Whatever that rock creature was – oh, what shall we call him? The Rock Man?'

'The Moon Man?' suggested Rory.

'Moon Monster,' said Amy.

'Rock Man it is, then. Whatever it actually is, it can transform anything it touches into moon rock. Some kind of sub-atomic virus, I should think. Or maybe quantum electron reversal. Or maybe . . .'

'I just want my dad back again,' interrupted Jess. 'Back to the way he was.'

The Doctor pointed a finger at her. 'Straight to the point. Good. Like that. Yes – but how *do* we change him back again?'

'We don't even know how he was changed in the first place,' Amy said. 'Or *why*.'

'Why?' Jess frowned.

The Doctor raised his finger. 'Good point, Amy. *Why* was the Rock Man changing things into moon stone? I mean, it seems to be unintentional. It didn't matter what the Rock Man touched, it was all transformed willy-nilly. Wall, car, door, furniture, even Ralph. So it seems to be an accidental side effect – it just can't help it.'

'Poor thing,' said Amy drily.

'It means there can't be any evolutionary purpose to it,' said the Doctor, thinking aloud. 'Which means that this creature isn't *natural*. It shouldn't exist . . .'

'But it does,' Rory pointed out.

'And this isn't helping get my dad back to normal,' Jess said. 'Isn't there anything you can do? What about that screwdriver thing?'

'It isn't a magic wand,' snapped the Doctor. 'I can't just zap him back to normal. We've got to think this through.'

'But we've got to *do* something,' Jess insisted. There was panic in her voice now.

The Doctor looked closely into her eyes. 'Jess, I know you're worried – but trust me. I'll find a way.'

Jess's eyes filled with tears. 'What if he dies?'

'The molecular transformation is rapid but pretty unstable. If we can find a way to halt the process in time then we can reverse it.'

'And how do we do that?'

'That's a good question,' the Doctor admitted. He looked at Rory and Amy. 'Any suggestions?'

He was met by blank, fearful looks.

'No?' The Doctor looked upset for a moment. But then he clapped his hands together and smiled. 'Right then. All down to me. Hush while I think. Wait – did somebody mention a cup of tea?'

'That would be me,' said Rory.

Rory started to move towards the kitchen, but Amy suddenly let out a yelp of alarm. 'Wait – look!'

She was pointed at Ralph Conway, still frozen solid in his armchair.

'I thought I saw Mr Conway move.'

'Dad?' said Jess, bending closer. She peered into the grey, sightless eyes. 'Dad? Can you hear me?' she whispered. And then, despairingly: 'It's impossible. He's like a statue.'

'Keep away, Jess,' said the Doctor firmly.

'But –'

Rory pulled Jess gently back. 'Best not to get too close if the Doctor says so.'

But Rory himself had stepped closer to Ralph's

chair. And in that second they all saw it happen – almost faster than the eye could follow, Ralph's stone hand leapt out towards Rory.

CHAPTER 12
FROZEN

Ralph's grey hand closed around Rory's jacket. Rory tried to pull away, but the grip was like a vice. He struggled and pulled, but there was no getting free.

And then Rory's jacket began to turn to stone. It whitened, and the material stiffened –

'Rory!' Amy screamed.

In a last, desperate motion, Rory twisted and turned and slipped his arms out of the jacket – just as it completed its transformation into moon rock. Held at arm's length by Ralph, the jacket immediately began to crack under its own weight. In an instant it fell to bits, scattering across the floor like a piece of dropped china.

And by now, Ralph was up and moving. He stood

stiffly, with an unearthly scrape of rock moving against rock. His head turned slowly to watch Rory as he cowered away, clinging to Amy. The colourless stone eyes seemed to narrow.

Jess was screaming. The sight of her father turned to stone was bad enough. Seeing him get up and move was almost worse.

Ralph was utterly blind to her distress. His attention was focused entirely on Rory and Amy.

The Doctor stepped up behind Ralph and aimed his sonic screwdriver. The tip flashed a brilliant green and a high-pitched whine filled the air, but there seemed to be no effect on the statue-like figure. The Doctor quickly tried several different settings, and eventually the statue's head twitched around to look at him.

'That's got your attention,' said the Doctor.

With a dull scraping noise, Ralph Conway turned and walked purposefully towards the Doctor.

'That's right – follow the pretty green light ...' The Doctor backed away, reversing out of the room, back towards the kitchen. He held the sonic screwdriver up, its emerald glow illuminating the darkened farmhouse.

Ralph followed him with heavy footsteps. The Doctor climbed backwards up a kitchen chair, onto the remains of the table, and out through the smashed doorway.

Ralph swept aside the wreckage and followed him outside.

The Doctor was in the farmyard now. Mist curled around his boots as he backed away from the Rock Man.

In the moonlight, Ralph Conway looked like a grim, white avenger. His pitiless gaze never left the Doctor as he trudged after him.

The Doctor circled around the farmer's Land Rover. That, too, resembled a stone carving – having been transformed into moon rock by the original Rock Man.

The Doctor sidestepped nimbly, putting the Land Rover between himself and Ralph. The farmer banged a stone fist down on the vehicle's bonnet in annoyance, cracking it like he had a sculptor's chisel.

The Doctor guessed it wouldn't take much for Ralph to smash the Land Rover into bits or just climb over it. He had to do something quickly. With a deft movement, he changed the frequency of the screwdriver again and aimed it squarely at Ralph.

The sonic screwdriver screamed and Ralph instantly froze.

'You did it!' Amy cried in relief. They had all followed them out of the house.

'Good old screwdriver,' said Rory. 'If you ask me, it is a bit magic.'

'Not magic,' snapped the Doctor. 'Just a carefully judged frequency modulation. The sound waves are vibrating the stone to a point where it cannot move. If I adjust the frequency by just one megahertz, the stone will shatter into a million pieces – and it's goodbye, Ralph.'

'Dad!' moaned Jess. 'Oh, Doctor – be careful!'

'I'm being *extremely* careful.' The Doctor moved cautiously forward, adjusting his grip on the screwdriver. 'But I can't keep him frozen like this all night. Rory, Amy – get some rope, anything you can, and see if you can tie him up.'

Rory went straight to the Land Rover, expecting to find a tow rope. But the vehicle was solid rock. There was no way to open it – and even then, he thought glumly, the contents might also have turned to stone.

'Try the shed,' said Amy, heading for the old wooden lean-to built against the farmhouse. Inside there were a number of tools – spades, garden forks, some musty cardboard boxes and a spare hosepipe. Coiled up on a hook was a long, blue, nylon washing line.

'Perfect,' said the Doctor.

Amy and Rory set about winding the line around Ralph's wrists and ankles, stretching it back and forth until he appeared to be caught in a giant, bright blue spider web.

'Be careful,' the Doctor said. He still had the sonic trained on Ralph. 'One crack and he could shatter.'

'What if he sort of . . . topples . . . over?' Rory

asked. 'Once you switch off the sonic he's free to move. But he's all tied up now and he might fall flat on his face.'

'Could be nasty,' agreed Amy.

Jess appeared, carrying a long length of heavy chain. She was shaking, tears streaking her face, but she was determined to stop any harm coming to her father. 'We can use this chain to secure him. If we wrap it around him a few times and then around the Land Rover, it should stop him falling over.'

They got to work and a little while later, with sore hands covered in rusty smears, they had secured Ralph to the Land Rover. The whole thing looked like some kind of weird modern art sculpture.

The Doctor clicked the sonic screwdriver off. The sudden silence seemed strange and frightening. Ralph Conway struggled to move – but was held fast by the nylon rope and chains.

The Doctor walked up to Ralph.

The Rock Man stared impassively back.

'Can you talk?' asked the Doctor.

But there was no reply.

'Might as well be talking to a statue . . .' muttered the Doctor.

The Rock Man continued to stare at the Doctor. Then it turned its head slowly to look at Jess and the others.

'He doesn't even recognise me,' said Jess sadly. 'There's nothing in his eyes. Just nothing.'

'He's not your father anymore,' the Doctor said.

'But can you turn him back again?'

'I don't know, Jess,' replied the Doctor honestly. 'I just don't know.'

CHAPTER 13
SAFETY IN SUNSHINE

They returned to the kitchen in a grave mood. 'Just look at this place,' said Jess despairingly.

The farmhouse was a wreck. There was broken furniture, crockery and fragments of moon rock everywhere.

'Yes,' said the Doctor eagerly. '*Look* at this place. Notice *everything*.'

'I think Jess is a bit upset, Doctor,' sighed Amy. The Doctor could seem so insensitive at times, it was embarrassing.

'Oh, don't worry about the farmhouse,' the Doctor told Jess. 'Bit of a tidy-up, lick of paint, you won't notice,' he ended lamely. 'Well, OK, maybe it'll need a bit more than that – but think of it as an opportunity. Maybe it was time you redecorated anyway. I mean, look at that wallpaper . . .' The Doctor pulled a disgusted face.

'Not helping, Doctor . . . ' whispered Amy.

Jess was just staring out of the window at her father.

Ralph Conway continued to pull and twist against his bonds.

The sky above was turning a strange colour. It was that time of night known as the false dawn – when things appear to be getting lighter, but sunrise is still an hour or so away.

The Doctor, Amy and Rory were trying to tidy up the mess. Jess didn't seem interested.

'She's more concerned about her dad,' Rory told the Doctor quietly.

'I know. And quite right, too. But still . . .' He turned on his heel, letting his sharp gaze wander over the debris in the kitchen. 'Look at this place. Notice everything. There's something I'm missing.'

'A clue?'

'It's not *Scooby Doo*, Rory.' Suddenly the Doctor banged the flat of his hand against the side of his head. 'Think, Doctor, think! Rory – cup of tea. Come on! I need tea to think. And biscuits – plenty of biscuits!'

Without another word the Doctor stalked out of the kitchen and plonked himself down in one of the armchairs in the living room. Then he closed his eyes and began to snore loudly.

'This is hardly the time for a snooze,' grumbled Rory.

'I'm thinking,' replied the Doctor, without opening his eyes.

'And snoring?'

'That's not snoring – that's the gears going round in my brain. Now shush and go and make that pot of tea.'

Rory went back into the kitchen where Amy met him with a frown. 'This place really is a mess. The Doctor's right, furniture can be replaced and walls can be repaired – but the dust is awful. It's absolutely everywhere. Look at my hands!'

She held them out for Rory to see. They were completely grey.

'Is is safe to touch the dust like that?' wondered Rory. 'Shouldn't you wear gloves or something?'

'The dust itself is completely harmless,' the Doctor called from his armchair in the other room. He still had his eyes shut.

'But it's so . . . sticky,' said Amy. 'It gets everywhere and stays there!'

Suddenly the Doctor leapt out of his seat and catapulted himself into the kitchen. 'Wait! Did you say it's sticky?'

He grabbed Amy's wrists and inspected her hands closely. 'Well, not *sticky*,' she said. 'Not sticky like a sweet or a lollipop is sticky. But it just sort of gets everywhere and coats everything . . .'

'Yes, of course,' said the Doctor, turning her hands this way and that.

Then he dropped to all fours and hunted around for some dust of his own. There was plenty. In another moment he was rubbing some of the fine grey dust between his own finger and thumb.

'Is there a problem?' wondered Jess.

The Doctor licked a finger and smacked his lips.

'Definitely moon dust. And yet . . . '

'I can't make a cup of tea with this,' complained Rory, holding up the kettle. 'It's covered in dust and it won't even rinse off.'

'That's it!' exclaimed the Doctor, leaping to his feet. He snatched the kettle from Rory. 'The dust is electrostatic. It carries a tiny, tiny electrical charge. Enough for each particle to be attracted to anything else nearby. I mean, moon dust – it's famous for it. How could I forget?'

'Perhaps you're not perfect after all?' Rory suggested gently.

The Doctor shot him a look. 'Don't be silly. Electrostatic dust. The astronauts on the *Apollo* missions had a terrible time with it. Got absolutely everywhere. Stuck to their boots, the joints on their spacesuits, moving parts on the lunar rovers. Nightmare.'

'But what does it mean?' asked Amy. 'We already know it's moon dust, after all. Comes from the moon rock, which is pretty much everywhere around here at the moment.'

The Doctor peered at her. 'Yes. Yes it is, isn't it?'

'So, what . . . ?' Rory prompted, taking the kettle back.

'Makes you wonder, doesn't it?' replied the Doctor with a curious smile.

'Wonder what?'

'If it's an invasion.'

'If what's an invasion?'

'All this!' the Doctor gestured grandly around them at the farmhouse wreckage. 'Perhaps this is some kind of alien invasion.'

'Oh, you'd love that, wouldn't you?' Amy said.

'No, wait, it can't be,' the Doctor said, suddenly changing his mind. His face fell. 'Pity though. At least then I'd know what was happening.'

'If it *was* an alien invasion,' said Rory, 'then they'd need to set their sights a little higher, wouldn't you say? I mean, no disrespect to Jess and her dad, but invading a small farm in the middle of England isn't exactly *Independence Day* all over again, is it?'

'Don't forget *War of the Worlds* started on Horsell Common – at least it did in the original HG Wells book.'

'Yeah, but that was just a story.'

The Doctor frowned. 'Was it?'

Rory looked doubtful. 'Well, yeah, At least I thought it was.' Living with the Doctor meant that he was now prepared to believe in almost anything.

The Doctor broke into a grin. 'Yeah, course it was a story. Only joking. Old HG Wells loved a good joke. Met him once, you know.'

'Really?' Rory was impressed. 'What was he like?'

'Bit of a pain to be honest. Gave him a few ideas for *The Time Machine* though.'

'I bet you did.'

'On the other hand,' the Doctor went on, '*Independence Day* actually *did* happen – but not until 2109 your time.'

'Oh.' Rory was frowning now. He never knew when the Doctor was pulling his leg.

'Doctor – look at this!' Jess was by the kitchen window. She pointed to where the Land Rover and her father stood outside, still bound by chains and washing line.

They gathered at the window. The sun was just coming up, sending rays of deep orange light across the dawn sky.

As the morning light touched the stone Ralph Conway, he seemed to flinch slightly.

'It's almost like the sunlight's hurting him,' said Jess.

'Not hurting him,' the Doctor said. 'Changing him. Look!'

Ralph had been struggling against his bonds. But now, as the first golden light of the new day touched his stone features, the man stopped moving. In minutes he was as lifeless as any statue.

The Doctor was already running out into the yard for a closer look. He circled around Ralph, watching for the slightest sign of movement.

Eventually, cautiously, he drew closer. Ralph didn't move.

The other joined him. 'Is he safe to be near?' asked Rory.

'Perfectly,' beamed the Doctor. 'It all makes sense now.'

'It does?' Jess didn't seem sure.

'Negative electrostatics,' nodded the Doctor.

'That's easy for you to say,' Rory smiled.

'It's a bit of a mouthful but that's how it works,' the Doctor replied. 'That's how the Rock Man can move around – and how Ralph can still move, even though he's made of stone. But ultraviolet light – such as sunshine – cancels the effect. Freezes the atoms where they are, so the thing's *completely* motionless.' The Doctor rapped his knuckles on Ralph's forehead.

'Hey,' said Jess. 'That's my dad you're tapping on the head.'

'I know.'

'You called him a "thing".'

'Sorry. Won't happen again.'

'Did you say ultraviolet light?' said Rory slowly. He was puzzling over something.

'Yeah. Sunlight. UV rays bombard the moon rock and –' the Doctor made a curious wriggling motion in the air with his fingers '*phhzzzzp*! Something amazing happens. But it means the Rock Men can only be active at night. During the day they're harmless.'

'Chris said he was researching into the effects of UV rays on certain kinds of minerals,' said Rory.

The Doctor clicked his fingers. 'That's it. That's it! Rory, you're wonderful. Amy, tell Rory he's wonderful.'

'You're wonderful,' Amy mouthed at Rory with a wink.

'I know,' he mouthed back.

'Now don't get all soppy on me,' warned the Doctor. 'I'm thinking and soppy stuff gets in the way of me thinking.'

'And what, exactly, are you thinking about?' asked Amy.

'That I need to speak to Chris, right now.'

'But we don't even know if he managed to get away from the monster.'

The Doctor huffed impatiently. 'He better have!'

Jess was already trying her mobile phone. 'There's no answer. It's not even connecting to Chris's mobile – like there's a signal problem or something. That's not unusual around here, I'm afraid. But, if he is still alive, I've a good idea where he'll be.'

CHAPTER 14
THE RESEARCH CENTRE

The sports car skidded to a halt and Amy flicked a strand of red hair out of her eyes. 'Not a bad ride,' she said.

The Doctor turned off the engine and smiled at her. 'Bit cramped,' he said. 'I prefer things to be slightly roomier on the inside.'

But the Doctor had, of course, relished the chance to drive Chris's car. 'It's only fair – he might want it back, after all,' was how he had explained it to Amy as he vaulted gleefully into the leather bucket seat behind the steering wheel.

The morning sunlight glinted off the red paintwork as they climbed out of the car. It was going to be a beautiful day – hopefully. Amy couldn't stop thinking about Ralph Conway. How did it feel to be turned into stone? Did he know what was happening? Did he know they were trying to help him?

Amy stretched her legs. It certainly had been a tight fit in that car. The Doctor had parked alongside a chain-link fence backed by thick bushes. There was no way to see what was on the other side and no sign of an entrance.

'Are you sure this is the right place?' Amy asked.

The Doctor pointed at a sign attached to the fence, half hidden by the foliage. It said:

HENSON RESEARCH CENTRE
NO UNAUTHORISED ACCESS
TRESPASSERS WILL BE PROSECUTED

'Not very welcoming,' commented Amy. She watched as the Doctor examined the fence. 'I suppose you'll want a leg up or something.'

'Something,' nodded the Doctor. He aimed his sonic screwdriver at the fence and the tip flashed green. A section of the chain-link quickly untwined and parted like a doorway.

The Doctor switched off the screwdriver and

smiled. 'After you!'

Amy stepped through the gap and the Doctor followed.

'Don't you think a big hole in their fence could be regarded as suspicious?'

'What hole?' asked the Doctor innocently, as he used the sonic to meld the links back together, zipping up the gap behind them.

'I sometimes think that thing must be magic,' said Amy, as the Doctor spun the sonic screwdriver and dropped it back into his pocket with a flourish.

'Or just superior technology,' he said. 'Amounts to the same thing to the untrained eye. It's simply a case of vibrating the wires in the chain link at the correct frequency to open them, and then reversing the polarity to close them.'

'Like I said – magic.'

'A pair of sliding doors would look like magic to a caveman.'

Amy raised her eyebrows. 'Oh, thanks – I'm no better than a caveman now, am I?'

'Well, you humans have come a long way in the

last few million years, but it pays not to get above yourselves.'

'Charming!'

The Doctor led the way through the bushes. 'Stop grumbling, Pond! Come and look at this!'

They emerged from the bushes by a tarmac path leading past a low, brick-built building. It was clean and modern, but with very few windows.

They crept quickly around the corner to a car park and a pair of large glass front doors. There was no one visible in the entrance foyer.

'That's odd – no receptionist and no security guards,' noted Amy. 'And yet there are cars in the car park.'

'It looks deserted,' agreed the Doctor, cupping his hands around his eyes as he peered in through the glass. 'Place like this should be busy. Lots of expensive equipment and top scientists – no one wants them standing idle.'

Amy pushed one of the doors open. 'It's not even locked.'

The Doctor followed her inside, ignoring the

vacant reception desk, and went straight through the foyer to the double doors at the rear. 'Hello!' he called down the corridor beyond. There was no reply.

'Doesn't look like there's anyone home,' said Amy.

The Doctor pushed open a door leading to an office. It was empty. Then he tried another door, this one marked with the word 'LABORATORIES'.

Beyond it was another corridor, this one lined with doors leading to various research labs. Each one had its own strange label.

'Spectography, mineralogy, geochemistry . . .' Amy read the signs on each door before opening them to reveal large rooms full of scientific equipment – but no people.

Computers whirred and indicator lights flickered on a variety of machines – but there was no one to read the gauges or take down the readings.

'It's like the *Marie Celeste*,' Amy said. 'Everyone's just . . . disappeared!'

'I hope not,' said the Doctor. 'I visited the *Marie*

Celeste. I don't want to go through all that again.'

Amy pushed open a door marked 'UV Biochemistry'. 'Um, Doctor, I think you'd better see this . . .'

Like the other labs, this room was full of scientific apparatus – work benches, computers and other complex machinery. There were a number of people – scientists, Amy presumed – seated at the various workstations and equipment.

But none of them were alive.

The Doctor stepped cautiously into the lab.

Hardly daring to breathe, Amy stayed in the doorway. The scene looked so strange and terrible that she didn't want to even enter the room.

The scientists stood peering into microscopes, or sitting at computer keyboards, utterly lifeless and unmoving – every one of them turned to stone.

'Just like Ralph Conway,' whispered Amy.

The Doctor was moving from scientist to scientist, checking them with his sonic screwdriver.

'No electrostatic activity at all,' he said grimly.

'They're completely motionless – dormant.'

Despite the Doctor's reassuring tone, Amy stayed in the doorway, unwilling to walk into what suddenly felt like a graveyard.

And then a heavy hand fell on her shoulder.

CHAPTER 15
WAITING

Rory was helping Jess to tidy up at the farmhouse. They had moved a lot of the rubble and moon stone and dumped it in the yard. Rory had picked up most of the broken furniture and put back anything that was usable where it belonged. The rest, the remains of it, he threw into the yard.

'You know, it's not as bad as it looks,' he told Jess, as he brushed the last chips of moon rock into a bin bag.

She raised an eyebrow. 'Really?'

'Most of this stuff is OK,' Rory said. 'The walls need a bit of rebuilding and re-plastering, but nothing a couple of good decorators couldn't handle in a day or so. And the rest . . . well, it just needs cleaning up.'

Jess sank into a chair. 'I hope you're right.'

Rory tied the bin bag and swung it out of the back door. 'You watch. By the time the Doctor and Amy get back, this place will look fine.' He hesitated, seeing that Jess wasn't convinced. 'Tell you what, let's take a break and have some breakfast.'

Rory found a toaster and a loaf of bread and set to work. Jess joined him in the kitchen, staring out of the window at her father. He still stood by the Land Rover, little more than a statue.

'Isn't there anything we can do for him?' she wondered.

'Not that I know of,' Rory replied. 'Maybe when the Doctor gets back . . .'

'Maybe we should have taken him to a hospital or something.'

'I don't think that would help. Believe me, I'd know – I'm a nurse. I used to spend all my time in hospitals and never once did I see anyone brought in because they'd been turned into moon rock. No one would have a clue what to do. Except the Doctor.'

'You really think he can help?'

'There's no one else I'd rather trust.'

Jess let out a sigh. 'I thought I could trust Chris – and look what happened there.'

'Don't be too hard on him,' Rory said gently. 'He was scared.'

'We all were – but he's the only one who ran away.'

Rory shrugged. 'Maybe that just shows he's cleverer than the rest of us. I wish I'd thought of it.'

'Don't joke. I'm supposed to be marrying him, remember.'

'People do a lot of stupid things before they get married,' Rory said, with some feeling. 'Don't be too hard on him.'

'Maybe dad was right. Maybe he isn't right for me.'

'Anything's possible,' Rory said. 'But at the end of the day, it's not your dad who's marrying him. It's you. Only you can decide.'

CHAPTER 16
WHAT WENT WRONG?

The hand felt unnaturally heavy. Amy spun around with a yelp, expecting to see the Rock Man towering over her.

But all she saw was Chris Jenkins.

He looked tense and scared – almost as much as Amy. His face was pale and drawn, with dark circles under his eyes.

'You just frightened the life out of me!' Amy yelled, swatting his hand aside. She felt relieved and angry at the same time. It didn't help that she could hear the Doctor laughing softly behind her.

'Look out!' the Doctor said, miming a big scary monster. 'It's *Chris*!'

Amy aimed a blow at his shoulder. 'Hate you.'

'Chris, glad you're here,' the Doctor said,

moving past her and shaking Chris by the hand. He looked dazed and confused as the Doctor peered closely into his eyes, as if searching for something deep within.

'Doctor . . . Amy . . .' Chris mumbled. 'How did you get here?'

'Oh, that was easy. Your sports car. Love it! Goes like the clappers, lovely motor.'

A frown twitched into view on Chris's forehead. 'How's Jess? Is she all right?'

'Yes, she's fine – apart from the fact that her dad's been turned to stone.' The Doctor looked around the lab again. 'A bit like your friends here.' He turned back to Chris, a steely look in his deep set eyes. 'Care to tell us about it?'

'Um, yeah. Yeah. That would be good.'

'So all that talk about analysing rock samples and handling moon rock – you knew something was already wrong,' said Amy a little later. They were sitting in a side room around a coffee table. It was some kind of rest area for the scientists, with a drinks machine and a small snooker table.

'Yeah,' Chris replied, sipping coffee from a polystyrene cup. He stared at the table in front of him. 'I'm afraid so.'

'Why didn't you speak up, then?' Amy demanded. She was annoyed with him. 'At the farmhouse. You could have said.'

'I was scared. I don't really understand what's going on – you see, I think it might be all my fault.'

'Why?'

'Part of the research we do here . . . well, there was a project, investigating the effects of UV rays on various kinds of rock.' Chris sighed and ran a hand down over his face. 'Including moon rock samples. It's something to do with NASA's preparations for the next moon landings. They need to control dust contamination. Our research was important – and top secret. I didn't want to start chatting all about it to strangers.'

'But still – even when that Rock Man attacked us . . .'

'I panicked. I just wanted to get away.'

'And you wanted to draw it away from Jess Conway,' interjected the Doctor. He was potting a red on the snooker table. The tip of the cue clicked against the ball and it shot straight into the corner pocket. 'Because you knew what it was after.'

The Doctor straightened up, rubbed the end of his cue with a piece of blue chalk attached by a string to the table, and smiled gently. 'You knew it was coming after you.'

Chris closed his eyes. 'When we started the experiments, the results were completely unexpected. The moon dust reacted in ways we couldn't have guessed at . . .'

'Electrostatic animation, cross-polarisation of the electrons at atomic level,' said the Doctor quickly. 'Yes, worked out all that for myself. The question is – what went wrong?'

'I don't know.'

The Doctor potted another red with a rattling stroke of his cue. 'Oh, come on, Chris. You must have a clue.'

'The moon rock had to be handled with extreme

caution at all times,' Chris said. 'The samples were kept in sealed cases. We handled them using gloves inside an airtight box. All the normal precautions. But one day . . . one of the insulated gloves tore. It must have been a sharp edge on one of the rock samples. I'm not sure. But the seal was broken.'

'That wouldn't normally be a problem,' remarked the Doctor thoughtfully, lining up another shot. 'Moon rock is pretty harmless.'

'That's what we thought. But we were wrong.'

'The people in the lab,' realised Amy sadly. 'Were they . . . infected or something?'

'Mutated,' Chris replied. 'It was horrible. Slowly at first – everyone was aware that they were getting heavier, stiffer . . . and then suddenly . . .'

'Sudden organic molecular reconfiguration,' finished the Doctor. He had cleared the table. He carefully placed the snooker cue back on the green baize surface. 'They never stood a chance.'

'And neither did Ralph,' said Amy.

Chris's head jerked up. 'What?'

'The Rock Man touched him, remember. Triggered the molecular change thingy.'

'Oh, no,' Chris buried his face in his hands. 'Not Ralph . . . What must Jess be thinking?' He stood up. 'I have to see her. She'll be distraught. Her dad's all she's got . . .'

'Wait a minute,' said the Doctor. 'Jess is OK. Her dad is OK – for the moment. The effect is unstable and I think the process can be reversed. But I need to know more about how it happened.'

Chris drew a deep breath. 'All right. What can I do?'

'Show us where the real work was done,' replied the Doctor without missing a beat.

Amy frowned. 'But I thought that was the lab . . .'

The Doctor shook his head. 'The work you say you were doing here – it would require at the very least a UV laser set-up, positively charged electron chambers and a nuclear particle tracker. There's nothing like the equipment necessary in there – and certainly no sealed unit.' He swung his gaze around to face Chris. 'So, come on, out with it: where's the top secret lab?'

CHAPTER 17
HOGGETT'S OFFER

There was a knock at the farmhouse door – or what remained of it.

'I'll get it,' said Rory. He went out to the kitchen and found a large, overweight man with a very red face standing in the doorway.

'Hoggett,' said the man as Rory appeared.

'I'm sorry . . . ?' Rory said.

'Who the Devil are you?' the man demanded, his thick eyebrows drawing down over a pair of small, but very sharp, eyes.

'Er . . . I'm Rory. I'm just visiting.'

'Where's Conway?'

Rory glanced out into the farmyard, where Ralph Conway stood immobile by the Land Rover.

'Come on, boy, spit it out,' demanded the man. 'He must be here somewhere. Tell him I want to see him!'

'Dad's not available right now,' said Jess, joining Rory. Her voice was cool, and Rory immediately got the impression that neither Jess or this rude visitor liked each other.

'This is Mr Hoggett,' Jess told Rory. 'You could say he's our next-door-neighbour. He owns the farm across the valley. And the farm next to that. And three farms beyond that.'

'Four,' Hoggett corrected. 'And it'll be five when I get this place.'

'And we keep telling you,' said Jess icily, 'that this farm isn't for sale.'

'It might not be on the market,' agreed Hoggett. 'But that doesn't mean it can't be bought.'

'My dad has already told you to back off, Mr Hoggett. We're not interested.'

'Well, we'll see about that,' said Hoggett. 'I've come to make a new offer. One that even someone as stubborn as your father would be hard pushed to refuse.'

'Look,' said Rory. 'This isn't a good time. As you can see . . . we've had a bit of bother and . . .'

Hoggett looked quickly around the kitchen, taking in the broken table, chairs, plasterboard and door frame. 'I can see that, boy. I'm not blind. And that's exactly why I've come. It'll cost a damned fortune to rebuild this place . . . money I know Conway doesn't have. If he can't afford to pay any workers, then he can't afford to pay for the upkeep of this place.'

'He'll find a way,' Jess argued – but she didn't sound convinced.

'Rubbish,' Hoggett scoffed. 'The place is falling apart – look around you!' He glanced around the kitchen and seemed surprised to find just how bad a state it was in. 'I mean, *look* at it! Place is falling apart!'

'Really,' Rory said, as firmly as he could manage. 'This isn't the right time.'

Hoggett gave him a withering look. 'I've come to speak to the organ grinder, boy – not one of his monkeys. Where is Conway? Don't tell me he's left you two in charge?'

'Dad isn't here at the moment,' Jess said patiently. 'Maybe if you could come back another time—'

'I'm not available at your father's beck and call, girl. Frankly I find it astonishing that Conway should leave the farm under the management of a young girl like you and her boyfriend.'

Jess glanced at Rory. 'Rory isn't my boyfriend.'

'I'm not her boyfriend,' Rory confirmed, just so there was no possibility of confusion.

Hoggett peered at him closely, lip curling. 'Oh, no. You're not. I'm thinking of that other oaf from town. Whatshisname. Jenkins. Always hanging around like a bad smell.'

'There's no call for that,' said Rory. He was beginning to get very fed up with this horrible man.

'Does *he* know you're seeing this fellow as well?' Hoggett asked Jess, jerking a thumb at Rory.

'I keep telling you, I'm not her boyfriend,' protested Rory. 'I'm not anyone's boyfriend. I'm married. To Amy Pond.'

'What are you blathering on about, boy? Sounds like you don't know what you're talking about half the time.'

'Perhaps you should just go.'

Hoggett seethed for a moment. 'Well, I can see it's pointless staying here unless I can speak to Conway.' He turned to Jess. 'Tell your father this is his final chance. He won't get a better offer. And tell him that statue he's had erected in the yard is damned ridiculous.'

'Statue?'

'Yes – the one with him chained to a Land Rover. Never seen anything like it! Damned ridiculous waste of money. The man's got far too high an opinion of himself.' Hoggett let out a loud *harrumph*. 'I never had a statue made of *me*.'

And with that, Hoggett turned and left without another word, stomping over the last bits of brick and dust left in the broken doorway. He stalked away across the yard, shot a dark look at Ralph Conway's "statue", and climbed into his Range Rover.

Jess watched him go and wiped a tear from her tired eyes.

'Don't get upset,' Rory said. 'He's just a . . . horrible man. Ignore him.'

'I can't ignore him, Rory. He's right. We can't afford to run this farm on our own. There's too much work to do for two people and we'd struggle to pay anyone to work here, even if they'd come out from the town.'

'I can see things were already difficult before . . . all this.'

'Dad knows he's going to have to sell the farm. He's not getting any younger. But he refuses to sell it to Hoggett. He practically owns the whole valley now.'

'I'm sure your dad will think of something.'

Jess smiled weakly. 'Thanks. I know you're trying to help, and you're very sweet.' She squeezed Rory's hand. 'Amy is a very lucky girl.'

CHAPTER 18
MINUS SEVEN

'The research centre extends far below ground level,' Chris explained. 'In fact, two-thirds of it is underground. The really top secret stuff – high level, fringe science research and development – takes place down on level Minus Seven.'

'That sounds brilliant,' said the Doctor, rubbing his hands together. He looked like a child about to walk into a sweet shop. 'Fringe science – my favourite kind!'

'What's fringe science?' asked Amy.

'All the sort of research that's on the very edge of known science,' Chris answered. They were walking along one of the corridors at the rear of the research centre, heading for the lifts that would take them down to level Minus Seven.

'All the stuff that's on the *fringe* of twenty-first century human science,' the Doctor corrected. He winked at Amy. 'They'll get there eventually.'

'I beg your pardon?'

'Nothing! Lead on.'

Chris stopped at the lifts, his shoulders slumping. 'There's really not much point. There's a problem I haven't told you about. The main lab on Minus Seven is locked and sealed.'

'Oh, that sounds even more interesting,' smiled the Doctor.

Chris, pale and sweating, met the Doctor's gaze. 'Doctor – you really, really don't want to go down there.'

But the Doctor's eyes were shining with curiosity now. 'Yes, I really, really do.'

They went down in the lift to level Minus Seven. There was a short, bare corridor leading to a set of heavy double doors. Each had a circular window made from frosted glass with the research company's logo etched into it.

'Not much of a barrier,' sniffed the Doctor, waving his sonic screwdriver casually at the doors. They clicked open immediately.

Amy screwed her eyes up as a gust of cold, dead air escaped with a quiet hiss. Beyond was a darkened concrete passage.

They stepped into the passage. Amy shivered. 'It's so cold down here – with all this concrete.'

The Doctor touched the wall. 'Not concrete, Amy – moon rock. The whole corridor is made from moon rock.'

'We shouldn't be here,' said Chris nervously.

'This is *exactly* where we should be,' the Doctor insisted.

He used the sonic screwdriver to light the way. It was very gloomy and at one point Amy stubbed her toe on something lying near the wall. 'Ouch!'

The Doctor shone the light on the floor, revealing a huddled grey shape. At first it looked just like a large rock or a stone, but then they saw that it was actually in the shape of a man – crawling along the floor. His face was frozen in a mask of fear.

'Oh, no,' Amy whispered.

The Doctor examined the stone body. 'Someone trying to escape,' he said quietly. 'Caught in the same transformation wave that turned this whole corridor to moon stone.'

'I told you it was a bad idea to come down here,' Chris said. 'We should go back now.'

'No,' said Amy. She tried to hide the shake in her voice. 'We've come this far. We have to find out what's going on.'

The Doctor smiled at her in the darkness and squeezed her hand. 'Come on, Pond,' he said.

Chris followed the Doctor and Amy to the far end of the passageway. Here there was a pair of heavy steel doors – or at least, they had once been steel. Now, they were rock. Grey stone rivets ran along the edges and the circular windows were useless.

'It's locked solid,' said Chris. 'There is no way through.'

The Doctor scanned it with the sonic screwdriver. 'All the internal electronics and locks have been turned to moon stone . . .' He fiddled with the screwdriver and pointed it at the centre of

the doors. The tip glowed a fierce green. 'However
– if I can break down the machinery . . .'

The sonic pitch rose to a scream and suddenly
there was a series of heavy clunks and cracks from
within the doors.

And a dark, black split appeared between them.

'Come on – brute force now.' The Doctor dug
his fingers into the split and started to heave.

Amy joined him, while Chris pulled at the
other door.

The stone doors ground slowly aside, releasing
a cascade of fine grey dust over the Doctor's head
and shoulders. When they had forced the doors
open just wide enough to step through, Amy
giggled. 'That's quite a dandruff problem you've
got there, Doctor.'

The Doctor brushed the dust from his hair and
stared into the cold darkness beyond the doors. 'It's
like opening a grave,' he said quietly.

Chris was shaking like a leaf. The Doctor aimed
his torchlight through the gap – and Amy let out a
sharp cry of despair.

CHAPTER 19

STONE SCIENCE

The huge, underground laboratory was impressive enough, but not exactly unexpected.

What took Amy by surprise was that everything – every computer, workstation, cable, monitor and control panel, right down to the last button and rivet – was made out of solid rock.

She had never seen anything like this. It looked like the world's most incredible, most complicated sculpture.

At the centre of the chamber was some kind of apparatus shaped like a giant, upturned spider. There was a round, central machine covered with technological components, with a number of thick support girders radiating out and up towards the ceiling.

The whole thing was surrounded by a number of heavy cables and power lines that trailed across the floor, plugged into various sockets and machines.

The Doctor stepped straight into the stone laboratory, his boots echoing around the cathedral-like space. His torchlight roved around the pale rock, picking out controls, computer banks – and then a man's face.

Amy gasped again – and then realised that, of course, the man was made out of rock. As still and lifeless as everything else down here.

'I'll never look at the moon in the same way again,' she said.

The Doctor examined the stone man. 'Caught in the transformation wave. Just like the others upstairs.'

'Did any of the scientists survive?' Amy asked Chris.

He shook his head. 'I'm the only one.'

The Doctor had moved to one of the main workstations. He scanned the computer with his sonic screwdriver, the green light playing eerily over the rocky surface. 'Everything is stored in here, all the research data, experiments, everything. But it's all turned to rock. The hard drives and flash memory – *everything* is rock.'

'Going to be hard to access any of the data, then,' Amy realised.

'Hard – but not impossible. There are some civilisations, mainly in the Pron-Kalunka Galaxy, that use granite as the base matter for all their technology.'

'And it works?'

'Yes, but it's very slow and a bit on the heavy side.' The Doctor knelt down, examining the edge of one of the computers very closely. 'But it *does* work. If I can just remove one of these memory sticks, I'm sure I could find a way to get the data out . . .'

'I don't like it down here,' Chris said. 'It all happened so quickly. The transformation was so fast . . . I was lucky not to be here when it happened.'

'Where were you?' Amy asked.

Chris gave a humourless laugh. 'I'd gone to start

up the UV generators. They're located in a side-room in the basement. It's not far from here – but far enough.'

The Doctor looked up, frowning. 'Start up the UV generators? That was lucky.'

'Not really.' Chris shuddered as he remembered. 'I heard it happen. Heard the shouts – the terrible grinding, cracking noise as anything and everything down here turned to stone. When I came back, I couldn't believe my eyes.'

'What did you do?'

'Ran around the research centre in a panic. No one else here was left alive.'

'What about the other scientists or their families and friends?' asked Amy. 'Didn't anyone enquire?'

'You have to understand that this is a top secret research project, Amy. Very few people know what we were doing or who was here. And the scientists are used to working down here without any contact with the outside world for days on end if they have to.'

'But even so . . .'

'Got it!' The Doctor waved a sliver of moon rock in the air. 'Flash drive from one of the main computers – now we can find out what happened!'

Chris swallowed. 'But I just told you what happened.'

'I mean what *really* happened,' said the Doctor.

Amy looked curiously at the stone flash drive. It looked like an ordinary memory stick – only grey. 'How are you going to use that? It won't work if it's turned to stone.'

'Oh, I know a few tricks – and I've always got this.' He produced his sonic screwdriver in the other hand. 'And your mobile phone, please.'

Amy sighed and handed over her phone. The Doctor sat cross-legged on the floor and got to work, opening up Amy's phone first of all and then using the sonic screwdriver on the memory stick. 'It's just a case of finding the right data transference code between the flash drive and the phone . . .'

'But how can the flash drive still work if it's been turned to stone?' wondered Chris.

'All memory sticks use silicon microchip

technology,' explained the Doctor. 'Silicon is a kind of rock. Now if I can create an interface between the chip and the display on the mobile . . .'

The sonic screwdriver hummed busily and the green light reflected from the Doctor's face in the darkness.

Amy wandered around the gloomy lab. There was just enough light coming from the corridor outside to see her way around. She stepped over rocky cables and around stone computer banks, exploring the strange machinery at the centre of the chamber. 'Is it safe to touch this, Doctor?'

'Oh yes, perfectly,' the Doctor replied without looking up from his work. 'The moon stone in here is all utterly inactive. It only appears to be the mobile Rock Men that have the ability to transform. Huh. There's a thought.'

'What?'

The Doctor concentrated on his task. 'What? Oh, nothing. Like I said – just a thought. Let me carry on thinking it for a second . . .'

Amy let her hand touch the stone machine, her

fingers gliding over the smooth, cool surface as she walked around it. It was very dark on the other side, opposite the entrance. She held out her hand in front of her, unsure what was ahead. Then she touched a lumpy, rough shape that definitely wasn't a machine.

A startled gasp escaped from her lips as she realised what was in front of her.

Towering over her in the darkness was a dark, humanoid silhouette – carved from solid moon rock.

The Rock Man.

CHAPTER 20
THE HEART OF STONE

The Rock Man glowered at her with sightless eyes. It was utterly still.

'What is it?' asked the Doctor, joining her quickly. He had been alerted by her sharp cry of shock. 'Ah. The Rock Man.' The Doctor scanned it quickly. 'Dormant – luckily for us.'

Amy backed carefully away from the massive figure. 'It's not like the others. You can tell the others were once people – scientists. But this is just all lumpy and . . .'

'Not quite alien,' finished the Doctor. 'It's something else entirely. Not human, not alien and not ordinary moon rock. And I think I know why.'

He held up Amy's mobile. The screen was scrolling through a huge amount of information.

'I hope you're not online,' Amy joked. 'That'll cost me a fortune.'

'No, this is information I've downloaded from the flash drive. Chris said they were researching into the effect of UV light on the electrostatic fields surrounding moon rock. That in itself wouldn't trigger all this . . .' The Doctor gestured around the stone lab, '. . . and it wouldn't account for our rocky friend here. There had to be something else – something the scientists hadn't bargained for.'

'And you've found it?'

'Yes – alien bacteria.'

'Ew.'

The Doctor's fingers wiggled around in the air, full of enthusiasm for his subject. 'Bacteria! Brought back from the moon in the rock samples. Not in every piece – maybe just one. But it's very unusual bacteria – it's 3.9 billion year-old bacteria, the remains of an ancient, extinct civilisation. It probably arrived on the moon in its infancy, on a meteorite –' the Doctor pounded a fist into his other hand to demonstrate the impact, '*boom*!

And it's been dormant ever since – trapped in the freezing dark on the airless surface of the moon. Some bacteria can live for decades – centuries even – and space-travelling bacteria even longer. Has to, if there's to be any chance of survival. And that's what this is all about – *survival*.'

'But now it's been brought to Earth from the moon,' Amy said, trying to follow the Doctor's train of thought.

'Yes, the *Apollo* astronauts must have picked up a piece of rock infected with this dormant space bacteria. It's been on Earth for years now – until suddenly the scientists here got hold of the rock and started bombarding it with ultraviolet light.' The Doctor's eyes lit up with excitement. 'And *bingo*!'

'The bacteria wakes up?'

'The bacteria wakes up!' The Doctor's expression hardened in the gloom. 'And it gets to work – controlling the electrostatic field contained in the moon rock, absorbing the UV rays and building itself a new body based on the first animal organism it's come into contact with in nearly four billion years.'

Amy's eyes widened. 'Human beings.'

'And so we have our lumpy Rock Man friend here.' The Doctor tapped the figure on the chest.

'But why change everything else into moon rock?'

'The bacteria is wild, uncontrollable. It's triggering molecular change at a fantastic, uncontrollable rate – trying to recreate an environment in which it feels at home.'

'So where's home?'

'Well, where's it been living for the past few billion years?'

'The moon.'

'Exactly. Good enough to call home now, I'd say.' The Doctor's deep-set eyes disappeared beneath a frown. 'But there's one question that remains.'

'Just one?'

'What on Earth does it want with Ralph Conway's farm?'

'I think I know the answer to that,' said Chris. It was the first time he'd spoken for some time. He was leaning against the doorway, partly silhouetted by the light outside.

'Yes,' said the Doctor. 'I should think you do.'

'The creature was after this,' Chris said. His voice sounded dull, as if he'd given up.

In his hand was a strangely shaped lump of grey rock.

'A piece of moon stone?' Amy queried.

Chris threw it to Amy. She caught it and then turned the rock around in her hands, angling it towards the light. 'It's shaped like a heart,' she said.

'Is this the original rock?' wondered the Doctor. He stepped closer and scanned the stone with his sonic screwdriver. The green light glinted off the grainy surface.

'Sample 247,' Chris said quietly. 'The Heart of Stone.'

'Figures,' said Amy.

'That's what we nicknamed it anyway. It must have contained the space bacteria you mentioned, Doctor.'

Amy gulped. 'Is it OK to handle it, then?'

'Probably,' said the Doctor. 'The meteorite was

only activated by UV light, remember. And it's done its work already. Helped make Rocky here come to life.'

The Doctor gestured towards the motionless Rock Man.

And as he did so, the Rock Man suddenly grabbed the Heart of Stone right out of Amy's hand.

CHAPTER 21
THE STATUE WAKES

'Rory,' Jess called from the kitchen. 'Come and look at this!'

Rory, alerted by the note of anxiety in Jess's voice, came at a run. 'What's up?'

'I thought I saw him move.' Jess pointed out of the kitchen window at her father.

Ralph Conway still stood by the Land Rover, bound to the vehicle by chains and washing line. He didn't appear to have moved an inch.

'It was probably your imagination,' he told her gently.

'It wasn't my imagination at all,' Jess protested.

'A shadow, then – maybe a bird flew overhead and you saw the shadow crossing.'

She shook her head. 'No, Rory. I definitely saw

him move!'

And then she pushed past him and ran out of the kitchen, heading across the yard to where her father stood like a statue.

Rory sighed and followed her out.

Jess came to a halt by the Land Rover and circled it. She stood in front of her father and looked up into his stone cold face. The eyes were open but unseeing. His hands were stiff where they gripped the chains.

Rory caught her up. 'It may even have been the sun – you know, the shadows changing as it moves.'

Jess shot him a look that said, '*Don't be stupid.*'

Rory had been on the receiving end of enough looks like that from Amy to recognise it easily.

'Negative electrostatics – that's what the Doctor said,' Rory pointed out. He wasn't completely sure what it meant but he could have a good guess. 'In other words, he can't move. The ultraviolet rays from the sun—'

'Oh, shush, Rory – use your eyes!'

Jess was holding her hand up towards her

father's rigid face.

Rory immediately grabbed her wrist. 'Don't touch him –!'

But then he stopped.

Because he'd seen something moving on Ralph Conway's stone face.

The eyelids were starting to close. With a tiny, thin scraping noise, his eyes blinked. Once. Twice.

'Get back,' Rory said, pulling Jess away.

But she yanked herself free and ran back to her father. 'Dad!'

Ralph's stone head twisted around to look at her. Every movement was accompanied by the sound of scraping rock.

'We should get away,' Rory insisted. His heart was beating faster. Where was the Doctor when you really needed him? Swanning around in a flash sports car, that's where!

Ralph Conway flexed his shoulders and turned to face his daughter. The stone eyes seemed to find her, but how he could see was anyone's guess. His lips parted, slowly, painfully, and Rory winced at the sound they made.

Ralph pulled at the chains that held him, shifting them, gripping them in his stone hands until each link was transformed with a dull crack into moon stone and snapped.

The chain fell away in ruins and the washing line parted, breaking into tiny, brittle pieces.

'Move,' said Rory, gripping Jess's hand and pulling her towards the farmhouse.

'No, wait . . .'

But Ralph had started to follow them with slow, plodding footsteps.

Rory half dragged Jess into the farmhouse. Once inside the kitchen he turned to close and lock the door – only to find that the door was already missing, along with part of the frame.

'Uh, we have a problem developing . . .' Rory muttered, as Ralph approached the door.

'What's he going to do?' asked Jess.

Rory snapped around, searching for something to use to defend themselves. He could hear the dull *scrape . . . scrape . . . scrape* of the man's approach behind him.

And then suddenly Ralph stood in the remains of the doorway.

Rory picked up the last remaining kitchen chair and faced Ralph like a lion tamer, holding the chair legs out towards him.

'Don't come any closer!' Rory told him, but his voice came out like a tight little squeak.

Ralph stepped into the kitchen.

'Oh, crumbs!' Rory backed away, keeping the chair up. 'Stay behind me, Jess.'

The stone man started walking towards them.

CHAPTER 22
RUN!

'Amy!' shouted the Doctor. Amy staggered backwards, horrified. The Rock Man lurched out of the shadows, its fist closed tight around the Heart of Stone.

'Not good!' yelled the Doctor, grabbing hold of Amy and helping her away. 'Not at all good . . .'

They tripped over a stone cable and crashed to the floor. The Rock Man stomped towards them.

'Up!' shouted the Doctor, hauling Amy to her feet.

They pelted across the room, dodging past moon rock workstations and under dangling stone power lines.

'This way!' cried Chris, calling them across the chamber as the Rock Man charged.

It crashed through a databank, hurling the thing to one side – where it smashed into fragments.

The Doctor, Amy and Chris ran, as moon rock shrapnel scattered across the floor.

'We've got to stop it,' the Doctor said, scrambling over a stone power converter. He helped the others climb over.

'Can't we just get out of here?' Chris asked.

'And let it come after us?'

Amy looked back to where the ugly shape of the creature loomed in the darkness. It didn't seem to care where it went or what it smashed to get to them. Clouds of grey moon dust were beginning to fill the chamber.

'What made it come alive again?' she asked the Doctor. 'I thought it was only ultraviolet light – sunshine.'

'The bacteria must be adapting,' replied the Doctor. 'The meteorite is learning to use any kind of energy source – including the sonic screwdriver. Look out!'

The Rock Man smashed the power converter

and strode through the debris.

The Doctor, Amy and Chris headed further into the depths of the secret lab – and further into the darkness.

The Doctor used the sonic screwdriver to light their way – the equipment here was packed closer together, linked by hundreds of wires and cables and junction boxes. It was like climbing through a stone jungle in the dark. The torchlight crept over the strange grey shapes as they picked their way through.

The Rock Man charged after them. It paused on the edge of the stone jungle, the dim light reflecting from its grey face. The deep holes that served as eyes were as black as night as they peered into the shadows.

The Doctor, Amy and Chris crouched behind a databank, hardly daring to breathe.

The Rock Man moved slowly forward, its heavy feet dragging across the stone floor with a harsh scraping noise.

The three of them remained absolutely still.

And suddenly the Rock Man heaved aside the databank, splintering the moon rock into a thousand dusty pieces, revealing the Doctor and his friends in an instant.

Amy screamed as she dived out of the way. The Doctor was right behind her, pulling Chris after him.

The Rock Man's massive hand swept down, crunching into the floor where the three of them had been a second before.

With a snarl of savage anger, the Rock Man charged after them. It thrashed its way through the power lines. The stone girders that helped support the central machinery crumbled.

There was a deep groan from above.

The Doctor's head snapped up and he shone his torch towards the ceiling. The huge stone ramparts that secured the machine stretched up into the shadows. Dust was falling like rain.

'It's going to destroy this place,' he realised.

Chris was appalled. 'It cost millions to put this lot together!'

'All a bit useless if it's made out of stone, though,' the Doctor pointed out.

There was a loud creak and fragments of rocks fell from above, scattering down through the machinery and onto the floor.

'We have to get out of here,' Amy said.

The Rock Man had almost caught them up. It shoved aside more computer workstations, leaving a trail of chaos.

The Doctor glanced up again. Then he turned to Amy and Chris. 'Head for the door – I'll meet you outside.'

'We can't leave you,' Amy protested.

'Just do as I say!'

Chris grabbed Amy's hand. 'Come on, Amy!'

The Doctor was already climbing onto the nearest workstation. From there he clambered across to a taller piece of machinery festooned with cables that snaked up into the branches of the central complex.

With a last, despairing look, Amy followed Chris, heading towards the exit. She had a horrible feeling she knew what the Doctor was planning.

The Rock Man saw Amy and Chris run – but the Doctor was still nearer. Craning its thick neck, the creature turned its pitiless black eyes up towards him.

The Doctor was hanging on to one of the support struts, leaning unsteadily out over the laboratory.

Letting go with one hand, the Doctor held his sonic screwdriver out at arm's length. He pointed it straight up into the shadows and activated it.

The tip glowed a fierce green and a shrill whine filled the chamber.

Something cracked like a gunshot in the darkness. The Doctor pointed the screwdriver in another direction and repeated the process. There was another huge crack – followed by a series of splintering noises. Dust cascaded from the ceiling.

Amy stopped at the doorway and looked up. The Doctor adjusted his aim again, and more dust rained down as a series of loud cracks echoed through the lab.

Everything started to shake.

'What's he doing?' Chris wondered.

'Using the sonic to vibrate the moon rock and crack it,' Amy said. 'He's going to bring this whole place down!'

The Doctor was climbing slowly down – he had to go carefully because the whole structure was shaking. He had the sonic screwdriver gripped between his teeth.

The Rock Man lumbered towards him, splitting a monitor bank in two with a scraping growl. Its hands reached out to grab the Doctor – but he was too quick for the creature.

He slipped down the last couple of metres, landed awkwardly and fell. The Rock Man's hands closed on dusty air.

The Doctor rolled along the floor, sprang to his feet and dodged past the creature. As he ran he held the sonic screwdriver out behind him and activated it.

A piercing whine shot through the air. The Doctor raised his arm, directing the sonic screwdriver straight up.

There was an almighty, splintering crack from above.

A huge piece of machinery dislodged from the ceiling and fell down, crashing into the rest of the apparatus below. Dust billowed out from the wreckage.

The Rock Man started after the Doctor.

The Doctor skidded to a stop by the door where Amy and Chris were waiting.

'When I say run,' panted the Doctor, 'run!'

They took one last look at the lab. The Rock Man roared and headed straight for them – and then the entire chamber shook as if gripped by an earthquake and the whole thing collapsed.

The central machinery cracked and fell into pieces, crashing down with a terrible noise. Sections of the ceiling tumbled after it, dragged down as the support legs gave way. Tons of moon rock crashed to the floor and a huge, thick cloud of choking dust rolled up.

The Doctor, Amy and Chris waited for the last

pieces to fall. The entire lab had been destroyed – there was nothing left now but a pile of rubble.

'Do you think that thing is dead now?' asked Chris.

'It was never truly alive – not in the way you mean,' said the Doctor sadly.

'But it's done for, isn't it?'

'I doubt anything could survive that,' said Amy.

The Doctor peered at the huge mound of grey waste. 'It must have been crushed,' he said. 'But look . . .'

Sticking out from the base of the wreckage, there was a rocky hand.

It still gripped the Heart of Stone.

The Doctor, covering his nose and mouth with a hanky so that he didn't breathe in the moon dust, crept back to the hand. He bent down and gently worked the stone loose.

'Why do you want that?' Amy asked.

'This rock is what started it all, remember,' said the Doctor. 'We don't want to leave it in the wrong hands.'

He wrapped the stone in his handkerchief and put it in a pocket. 'Come on – let's go.'

Pieces of moon rock continued to fall, clattering down through the debris. Dust swirled.

And, faintly, the Rock Man's fingers began to move . . .

CHAPTER 23
EXPLANATIONS

Rory tried to position himself in front of Jess. He wasn't sure this was a very good idea, but it felt like the kind of thing he should do.

The Rock Man – in the shape of Ralph Conway – continued to approach.

And then Jess stepped past Rory and held out her hands to her father.

'Dad,' she said. 'It's me – stop.'

And, remarkably, Ralph Conway did stop.

'Don't get any closer,' hissed Rory. He didn't want to see Jess turned to stone as well.

But a very strange thing was happening. Jess was inching closer to the stone figure before her. And he was staying absolutely still.

'Be careful,' Rory insisted.

'I think it's OK,' Jess whispered. 'Really, I do . . .' She took another step.

Ralph Conway's head dipped slightly lower, as if he was about to say something.

'Dad?' Jess said gently.

Ralph's grey lips parted slightly and a horrible scraping sound emerged. It looked like he was trying to speak, but it was causing him terrible pain.

'It's all right,' Jess said. 'Don't try to talk. I understand.'

'You do?' said Rory.

'He doesn't want to hurt us,' Jess said. 'Look at him. He's terrified.'

'Look at *me*,' said Rory. 'I'm terrified too.'

Ralph fell silent. He remained completely still.

Encouraged, Rory came a little closer. Every line in Conway's face, every tiny bit of stubble and mark on his skin, was perfectly captured in stone. It was astonishing – more than a work of art, in fact. There was no man-made sculpture in the world like this.

'We'll get you back, Dad,' Jess said softly. She

turned to Rory. 'Won't we?'

'Yeah, of course.' But Rory couldn't for the life of him see how.

There was an abrupt knock at the door – or rather the door frame. Rory and Jess had hardly turned their heads before Mr Hoggett strode uninvited into the farmhouse.

'Door was open,' he explained snootily. 'In fact, the door was missing. Like half the rest of this dump. It's in a state of collapse, you know.'

'I thought we'd seen the last of you, Mr Hoggett,' said Jess.

'The only way you'll see the last of me, my dear girl, is when you agree to sell this hopeless excuse for a farm.' Hoggett smiled wolfishly.

Then something else caught his attention. Hoggett's face darkened as he saw Ralph Conway.

'I can't believe you brought that awful thing inside,' he said. 'But then I suppose it's better than having it on display outside. Always thought Conway had too high an opinion of himself – but a *statue*, for goodness' sake!'

The statue's head turned slowly and glared at Hoggett.

Hoggett practically choked.

Jess and Rory watched him turn pale, then red and then almost black with fury.

'What . . .' Hoggett spluttered, 'what on Earth is this meant to be? Some kind of joke?'

'Well,' began Rory, and then stopped. He couldn't think of anything to say.

'Explain!' thundered Hoggett.

'It's really very simple,' said the Doctor, sweeping into the room unannounced.

Every head snapped around to look at him and Amy. Every head except Ralph Conway's, which turned slowly with a harsh grinding noise.

Chris Jenkins appeared in the door frame behind Amy.

'Chris!' exclaimed Jess, her voice full of shock and delight – and a hint of uncertainty. 'Chris? Are you all right?'

'I'm not sure,' he replied.

Hoggett continued to splutter with indignant

anger. 'What's going on? Who are these people? What's happening?'

'Hello,' said the Doctor, waving his fingers briefly at the irritated man. 'I'm the Doctor, this is Amy, that is Chris – Jess's fiancé – and that is Rory – Amy's husband – I know, it's beginning to get confusing, but don't worry, all will become very clear in a moment.' The Doctor clapped his hands together with some satisfaction.

Hoggett pointed a trembling finger at Ralph Conway. 'And this?'

'This is Ralph Conway, Jess's father,' the Doctor explained patiently.

Hoggett's finger continued to tremble, but it was impossible to tell whether this was due to fear or anger. 'I know *who* it is . . .' he said through gritted teeth.

'Ah,' realised the Doctor. 'You're wondering why he appears to be made of stone.'

'But –'

'That's because he is, in fact, made of stone.'

'But –'

'And not just any old stone,' the Doctor continued brightly. 'But *moon* stone. That's rather extraordinary, don't you think?'

'But –'

The Doctor let out an exasperated sigh. 'But what?'

'But it *moved*!'

'Ah, yes,' the Doctor nodded slowly. 'That is the *other* extraordinary thing. Isn't it wonderful that one day could be so full of so many extraordinary things? They're the days I love best, to be honest.'

Hoggett was seething. 'Will someone please explain *exactly* what is going on here?'

There was silence as everyone looked at the Doctor.

'That would be me, then,' said the Doctor. 'Well, as I said, it's really quite simple. It started when a meteorite crashed into the surface of this planet's moon nearly four billion years ago. Lovely big crater, tiny little something left at the centre. An alien something. Carrying alien bacteria. Special alien bacteria that lay on the cold, airless surface of the moon until an unsuspecting astronaut from the last *Apollo* mission collected it as part of a sample of moon rocks to bring back to Earth for study. All clear so far?'

Silence.

'Good, I'll carry on. We're getting to the good bit! Not all the moon rock samples were tested straight away. Some were, some were given away as presents to foreign governments and some were kept for display. Some were held back for further investigation. And some – including the one carrying our special alien bacteria – were sent for analysis by Chris and his friends here at the Research Institute.'

Chris gave a little wave.

'Chris and his friends bombarded the moon rocks with ultraviolet light – and the special alien bacteria reacted. This is what it had been waiting 3.9 billion years for. So, it reacted pretty quickly, because, let's face it, it had been waiting for a long, long time and was getting pretty impatient. And it used its own unique and special talent: to change whatever it touched into something that it could use as a body.'

'Change?' said Hoggett.

'Molecular reconfiguration,' nodded the Doctor. He wiggled his fingers together in a complicated pattern as he spoke. 'Transforming metal, plastic, wood, skin, bone, *anything* at all, into moon rock.'

'And your point about the moon bacteria is?' prompted Jess.

'It's natural. It can't help what it does. You humans always wanted to fly, and it took you ages to *make* gliders and wings and engines and build something you could fly *in*. But the birds and the bees have been doing it since forever. *Naturally*. They can't help it. And that's just like the moon bacteria. It can't help changing things.'

The Doctor turned in a slow circle, ensuring everyone was still listening. Hoggett's mouth was hanging open, and the Doctor reached out and gently closed it.

'The bacteria copied the first real life form it discovered, fashioning a humanoid body for itself.'

'The Rock Man,' said Amy.

The Doctor nodded thoughtfully. His dark eyes

glowered from beneath his heavy brow. 'And then. Then it went looking for something.'

CHAPTER 24
CHRIS'S SECRET

'Looking for what?' asked Rory. 'Sorry, I'm not following this at all.'

The Doctor smiled. 'It went looking for a particular rock: the lunar sample that had started it all. The source of the bacteria.'

'Which was where?' asked Jess.

'Here,' answered the Doctor. 'In the farmhouse.'

'But – how?'

'Ask Chris.'

Jess turned to Chris with a puzzled frown. 'Chris?'

Chris looked uncomfortable. 'I . . . brought it here. From the research centre. I'm sorry, I really didn't know what I was doing. But I knew the rock was trouble. I'd seen the effect it had produced at the research centre, turning everything and everyone I knew into moon stone. I was scared. But I knew I had to get the rock away from the centre, in case it happened again. So I hid it here.'

'You never told me.'

'I didn't want to frighten you. I was trying to think of a way to deal with everything. I'd only just got your Dad to accept me – almost, anyway – and I didn't want anything to risk that.'

Jess looked at her father, still turned to stone. 'I think you risked *everything*.'

'Possibly,' the Doctor agreed. 'But Chris really didn't know what he was dealing with. And he couldn't have known that the Rock Man would come looking for the stone – which, incidentally, I have here in my pocket.'

He took the heart-shaped lump of rock from his jacket pocket.

'You mean that's what brought the Rock Man to the farm?' asked Jess.

'Yes. He arrived in the middle of the night, knocked down your wall – accidentally changing it into moon rock – blundered around a bit and then got scared off by your father.'

'I came straight away,' Chris continued. 'I wanted to take the Heart of Stone back – or at least, away from here.'

'Heart of Stone?' queried Rory.

The Doctor held up the rock. 'Yeah, looks a bit like a human heart. Complete coincidence. In fact, it doesn't really look like that at all.'

He produced the sonic screwdriver in his other hand and pointed it at the rock. The tip shone green and a shrill noise filled the room. Suddenly, the rock cracked and disintegrated in a puff of grey dust that trickled through the Doctor's fingers.

The Doctor snapped the sonic screwdriver off. Left in his other hand was something a little smaller than the original rock – something smooth, spherical and black. It was about the size of a tennis ball, but glossy, like a hugely magnified droplet of oil.

'What is it?' asked Rory, his eyes wide.

'This is the original meteorite that struck the

moon all those millennia ago.' The Doctor held the sphere out for them to see. 'It's from another galaxy altogether. Here, catch.'

The Doctor tossed the ball casually to Mr Hoggett, who caught it instinctively. He looked at the ball and then at the Doctor, opening and closing his mouth but not making a sound.

The Doctor smiled. 'The moon rock was just the outer layer, thickening around that ball over billions of years.'

'I left the Heart of Stone here, hoping to hide it until I worked out what to do,' said Chris. He looked miserably at Jess. 'I'm sorry.'

'The Rock Man came back the next night, while you were here,' Jess said. 'You knew what it was and why it was here. And yet you ran away.'

Chris looked shamefaced, but the Doctor said, 'Actually, Chris saved us all last night, Jess. He took the meteorite away with him, knowing the Rock Man would follow him – and leave you alone.'

'But not before the Rock Man had smashed the place to bits and done *that* to my dad!' Jess pointed at her father, who stood like a statue in the middle of the room.

'And that's where the good news comes in,' said the Doctor brightly. 'I'm pretty sure we can change your dad back to normal.'

Jess stifled a sob. 'How?'

'Using the meteorite.' The Doctor plucked the black sphere out of Mr Hoggett's hands. 'The change is highly unstable – it's constantly on the edge of being permanent. But that means it's also right on the edge of being temporary. If I can tap into the molecular code contained in this meteorite and reverse it, everything should turn out hunky-dory.'

'Did you really just say "hunky-dory"?' laughed Amy.

The Doctor winced. 'It won't happen again, I promise.'

Jess had turned to Chris, wiping away a tear. 'Is it true? Can he get Dad back to normal?'

Chris nodded. 'If the Doctor says he can, then I believe him. And so should you.'

'It may take a few minutes to calculate the code,' said the Doctor. He cleared a space on the kitchen table and sat down. 'It's probably some kind of binary-electron code – something natural and basic . . .' He fished in his pocket and produced a jeweller's eyeglass, which he screwed into place so that he could examine the meteorite in minute detail.

Chris took Jess by the hand. 'Do you forgive me, Jess? I'm sorry for the trouble I've caused.'

'Why didn't you tell me what was going on in the first place?'

'I didn't think you'd believe me. And worse than that – I thought you might call the engagement off. Or your dad would.'

Jess touched his cheek tenderly. 'I just wanted you back, Chris, that's all.'

At this point the Doctor looked up from his work. 'You know, this is a very difficult job and requires total concentration. A little quiet would help. You can save the soppy stuff for later.'

Jess smiled and squeezed Chris's hand. 'Anything

you say, Doctor.'

'Good.' The Doctor clicked open his sonic screwdriver. 'Now, complete silence, please.'

His only answer was a terrific crash from the remains of the kitchen doorway – and the sight of the Rock Man looming through the gap, grey hands outstretched . . .

CHAPTER 25
THE DOCTOR CHANGES

'Oh, not you again,' complained the Doctor. 'What the dickens is *that*?' roared Mr Hoggett as the Rock Man stepped into the farmhouse.

Everyone backed away quickly – everyone except the Doctor, who jumped to his feet and walked swiftly towards the creature, his sonic screwdriver at the ready.

'Hello . . .' he began.

The Rock Man gave a gravelly snarl.

'I'm so glad you survived the – er – rockfall,' continued the Doctor. 'And I thought you'd probably come after me. Or rather – this.'

In his other hand he held up the glossy black sphere.

'I've just been having a bit of a tinker,' the

Doctor confessed. 'You know, trying to see what makes it tick and how I might use it to return poor Mr Conway back to his usual self . . .'

The Doctor pointed at Ralph Conway.

The Rock Man's dark eye-pits turned towards the stone farmer. Its jaws scraped together as it seemed to consider.

'You see, we have a communication problem here,' the Doctor went on. 'I can't understand a word you're saying. My guess is that your species has been mutated so far from its original form that it's *beyond* alien. It's something completely new and unique.'

The Rock Man growled.

The Doctor regarded it sadly. 'It's not even like you're a long, long way from home. You don't even *have* a home.'

The Rock Man growled again, and the noise was like a paving slab being dragged over concrete.

'What can I do to help?' the Doctor asked.

Everyone watched in amazement as the Doctor stood calmly before the towering grey creature, looking directly into the deep, dark pits where its eyes should be.

He was close enough for the creature to reach out and crush him – or turn him to stone.

And then the Rock Man did reach out.

And pointed a stubby, rocky finger at the Doctor's own hand.

The hand that held the meteorite ball.

'Yes,' the Doctor whispered. 'I think I understand.' He held the ball up slowly. 'This is your home?'

The Rock Man leaned forward and, very carefully, touched the ball.

It was impossible to tell exactly what happened in that moment.

There was no flash of light, no spark, no crackle or rumble of thunder.

But somehow, something – everything – changed in that moment. It was as if a connection had been made with something strange and mysterious – a connection between the Rock Man and the Doctor.

The Doctor stiffened – literally.

The hand that held the meteorite turned rigid, pale.

And then grey, like moon rock.

'Doctor!' gasped Amy.

The sleeve of the Doctor's tweed jacket changed to grey, the elbow patch stiffened and turned to stone.

'Oh, my goodness,' breathed Jess. 'No, please, no – not again . . .'

The Doctor turned his head to look at the others. His deep eyes blazed with fierce intent, the incredible mind behind them burning with the effort of speaking. 'Don't do anything – don't do anything at all,' he said gruffly.

And then his eyes turned solid.

The dreadful greyness had seeped up his neck and turned his face into a pallid, eerie stone. His hair whitened like that of an old man and stiffened, the heavy fringe apparently carved from solid rock.

In less than a few seconds, the Doctor had been completely transformed. He stood like a statue, holding the meteorite ball, with the Rock Man still touching it.

Amy held Rory tightly and screamed, '*Doctor*!'

CHAPTER 26
ATHROCITE

The Doctor had been transformed entirely into moon rock.

His head turned slowly towards his friends with a terrible grinding noise. And then his grey lips parted in a smile.

'It's all right,' he said. His voice sounded dry and gravelly, completely unlike normal. It was a sound that made the hairs on Rory's neck stand up and he felt Amy's body wilt next to him.

And yet . . .

And yet the Doctor was smiling – sort of.

It wasn't easy to tell with his features turned to stone, but the lips were definitely smiling, even if there was a vague look of pain in his flat, grey eyes.

'It's OK,' he rumbled again. 'I'm fine. Really.'

He raised his arms, spreading the fingers of his rock-like hands.

'Well, not exactly *fine*,' he ground on, 'not fine in the *normal* sense . . .'

He stepped slowly forward, arms held awkwardly as if trying to maintain his balance in a body that must have felt so strange and heavy. His grey boots clumped across the carpet as he approached Amy and Rory.

'I mean – look at me!' The stone Doctor examined his own hand closely. 'I'm made of moon rock! Moon rock moving using negative electrostatic energy. Isn't that *amazing*?'

'It is . . . amazing,' Rory agreed. But he looked very uncertain.

'Amazing,' Amy echoed. 'But not what we expected. Or wanted.'

'It's all right,' the Doctor insisted.

He was trying to sound reassuring, but the harsh, scraping tones sounded totally alien coming from the Doctor.

'I knew this would happen,' the Doctor told them. 'Sort of. Well, more of a guess, really.'

'What on Earth have you done?' Amy finally blurted, unable to stop herself. She put her hands up to her face, blinking away tears.

'Don't get upset,' urged the Doctor.

He reached out for Amy but she recoiled. 'Don't touch me! I don't want to be turned to stone!'

But the Doctor had reached a little too far – and started to topple over. He moved quickly, for someone made out of rock, and regained his balance. 'Whoa! Gotta be careful here. One slip and crack! I'll go all to pieces.'

'Doctor,' said Jess. 'What have you done?'

The Doctor turned slowly and carefully to face Jess. 'Only the most incredible and amazing thing I've done so far today. And I try to do something like that almost every day. I've been turned to stone.'

'We can see that.'

'So, now I know what it's like to be like your dad. Or the Rock Man here.' The Doctor pointed to the towering creature behind him.

The Rock Man was simply watching the Doctor through its shadowy eyes, as if wondering what he might do next.

'But Dad can't move or speak – at least, not properly.'

'That's because he's only human,' replied the Doctor. 'I'm something else. And so is our friend here. We can use the negative electrostatic energy to move more easily. Well, a bit more easily. And that's not all.'

The Doctor turned and said something to the Rock Man. But not in English, or any kind of language anyone else in the room had ever heard. It sounded more like one slab of concrete being pulled across another.

And the Rock Man replied in kind.

'Can you two understand each other?' asked Amy.

The Doctor nodded slowly. 'Absolutely. Athrocite here can finally communicate. And I can only understand him because I now share the same molecular structure. It's a complicated and totally unique way to talk.' The Doctor's stone hand reached up to touch his stone throat. 'Plays hell with the vocal chords, mind you. Especially when they're made entirely of stone.'

'So, what's he saying?' Amy wanted to know.

'And did you just call him by his *name*?' Rory asked.

'Yes. I'm calling him Athrocite. I don't know if it's his actual name or the name of his original species. But it seems nicer than Rock Man.'

'But what's he actually saying?' Amy insisted.

The Doctor bit his stone lip. 'What he's saying is this: "how can I get away from this dreadful place?"'

There was an uncomfortable silence.

'Or words to that effect,' the Doctor added nervously. 'Place . . . planet . . . it's difficult to be certain. And it loses a little in translation.'

Athrocite snarled something and the Doctor nodded. 'Yes, yes, I'm trying to explain . . . Keep your hair on. Not that you've actually got any.'

'For Heaven's sake,' snarled Mr Hoggett, his face

redder than ever. 'No one invited him here. Fellow's some kind of monster if you ask me.'

'I didn't,' said the Doctor pointedly.

'Or is this just some kind of stupid practical joke?' Hoggett demanded to know. His lips twisted into a sneer of contempt. 'You look like a student.'

'It's not a joke,' said the Doctor. 'And I'm not a student.'

'Because it's not in the least bit funny,' Hoggett continued.

Athrocite rumbled something else.

'Athrocite says he never meant to come here,' the Doctor translated. He took the ball from Athrocite's hand. 'His distant ancestors arrived on the moon in this meteorite. Scientists experimented on the meteorite and it formed a new kind of life, roughly based on a human being. In other words – Athrocite was born. So far, so good. But anything he touched was transformed into the same material. The research lab, the scientists, anything at all. Disastrous. And it won't stop there. The process is highly unstable – there's no way to control it, and if we don't find a way to stop it . . .'

'What will happen, Doctor?' asked Amy.

The Doctor's tone was deadly serious. 'It won't stop – ever. It'll keep on going, transforming, until everything and everyone and everywhere is made of moon rock.'

CHAPTER 27
SHUT UP, HOGGETT!

'Everything?' said Amy. 'We have to find a way to stop it – to get Athrocite away from here. Away from the planet.'

But Athrocite was growing impatient – a dark maw opened in his craggy face, releasing a grating howl. He seemed to loom taller in the room and the others backed quickly away.

'Please,' the Doctor pleaded with the Rock Man. 'You must understand – I'm doing my best to help you. But time is running out and I have to explain . . .'

Athrocite swept angrily at the air and the Doctor jerked backwards, raising his hands. 'Steady!'

The creature roared and stretched out, past the Doctor's head, snatching at Rory.

Rory darted backwards, Amy holding onto him all the time. 'What does it want?'

'The meteorite,' said the Doctor.

And then he turned back to Athrocite. 'Calm down – I want to help but you must be patient!'

Athrocite snarled again and stepped towards Rory.

'Should I hand it back?' Rory asked, holding the meteorite close to his chest as he looked uncertainly at the Doctor.

'Not yet.' The Doctor pointed the sonic screwdriver at the Rock Man. 'I'll use this if I have to, Athrocite!'

The creature turned its baleful, empty eyes on the Doctor.

The Doctor triggered the sonic screwdriver – but nothing happened.

Like the Doctor, the sonic screwdriver was now made entirely of moon rock.

'There's plenty more where that came from,' warned the Doctor helplessly.

'What the Devil are you trying to do?' asked

Hoggett. 'It's had absolutely no effect!'

The Doctor glared at him. 'I can see *that*,' he hissed. 'I had hoped to freeze him for a second or two, but . . .'

Athrocite glowered at the Doctor, eyeing the sonic screwdriver with suspicion.

'Get on with it, then!' seethed Hoggett. 'Drive him away! Keep prodding him with that thing and it'll drive him away!'

The Doctor tried to run a hand through his hair in exasperation, only to find his hair was all made of stone as well as the sonic screwdriver and his fingers only scraped noisily across his head. His grey eyes glared at Hoggett. 'You just don't get it, do you? This creature is *totally* unique. And frightened. That makes him dangerous – he's massively powerful, but he's struggling to contain it. What if he decides he's had enough? Or panics? He could turn everything and everyone here to moon stone in an instant. And then the farm. And the surrounding countryside. When will it stop? The rest of the country? The whole planet?'

The Doctor's voice was raised now and both Amy and Rory could see that he was under intense pressure to resolve the situation.

Athrocite kept watching the Doctor, and then Hoggett, and then the Doctor again as the argument went back and forth.

But Hoggett didn't seem to care – or understand. He rounded angrily on the Doctor, his face reddening. 'If you know so much about all this, why don't you just explain to the wretched thing that it's not welcome here?'

'Athrocite doesn't entirely trust me – or any human being,' the Doctor replied. 'And why would he? He's *completely* alien to your world – he's something entirely new, with origins in the dawn of time.' He turned and looked up at Athrocite, his tone softening. 'In fact, it's a privilege just to be standing here.'

Hoggett spluttered. 'A privilege? You don't know what you're blathering about, man!'

'Doctor,' interrupted Amy. 'What can we do? How can we help him?'

'I had hoped to persuade him to come with us in the TARDIS – to take him to another planet, somewhere in the Pron-Kalunka Galaxy where there are lots and lots of silicon-based life forms.'

Athrocite was growing impatient again, a long, low, scraping growl escaping from deep within his rocky torso.

The Doctor turned and spoke to him in his own language, and the two of them exchanged a number of strange, unearthly noises.

'Well?' asked Amy. 'Will he do it?'

'He wants to know what's wrong with *this* planet,' replied the Doctor.

'Nothing,' said Amy. 'Except that it's ours.'

'But Athrocite doesn't have a planet of his own, Amy. What's the difference?'

'I've had just about enough of this,' Hoggett erupted. 'The thing is made of rock. Why don't you just take a ruddy great sledge hammer to it?'

'*I'm* made of rock!' the Doctor objected. 'Do you want to take a sledge hammer to me too?'

'Yes!' Hoggett yelled. Then he turned to face

Athrocite. 'I don't know who or what you are, because none of this makes the slightest bit of sense to me – but I do know this: you don't belong here, you're not wanted here, and you –'

Hoggett froze mid sentence.

His face stiffened.

He turned grey, greyer . . . and with a sharp cracking sound he turned to solid stone.

There was complete silence. Everyone simply stood and looked at him.

Ralph Conway had reached out and gripped Mr Hoggett's shoulder from behind. The effect of the touch had been instant – Hoggett had been transformed into moon rock.

'Dad!' said Jess, a hand to her mouth in shock.

'Thank goodness someone found a way to shut him up,' said the Doctor. 'What a very annoying man. Did anyone else think he was a very annoying man?'

Everyone else nodded immediately.

And then Rory said, 'Um, Doctor . . . Athrocite seems to have left.'

The Doctor snapped around. The Rock Man had vanished.

CHAPTER 28
'NOT A SECOND TO LOSE!'

'No!' cried the Doctor, rushing out of the farmhouse. 'No, no, no!'

Rory and Amy ran out after him, closely followed by Chris. 'Where did he go?'

'There!' The Doctor pointed.

Athrocite was stomping away across the yard.

'Come back!' the Doctor yelled.

Athrocite turned slowly around, eyes narrowed. A low growl scraped out of his mouth.

'Maybe that wasn't such a good idea,' said Amy.

The Doctor darted forward, slipped, nearly fell, scraping his hand along the brickwork of the wall.

'Be careful!' Chris told him. 'You're made of rock, remember! If you fall and break –'

'Good point,' agreed the Doctor, regaining his

balance.

'Athrocite looks *really* angry,' said Rory.

'Between him and Mr Hoggett, it's a wonder we're all still standing,' said Amy. 'I've never seen such bad tempers.'

'At least Athrocite has an excuse,' said the Doctor.

'True,' agreed Rory. 'But he doesn't have this.' He held up the meteorite ball.

The Doctor leapt over to him, regardless of the risk. 'Rory! That's brilliant! You've still got the meteorite!'

'It's what Athrocite wants, isn't it?'

'Definitely,' nodded the Doctor. 'Probably. Maybe. Let's hope so. Quickly – back inside the farmhouse.'

Back inside the kitchen, the Doctor took the meteorite ball and put it down on the table. 'This might be just what we need.'

'I thought you said Athrocite needs it?' said Amy.

'He does – the negative electrostatic field that allows him to move, and me and Ralph and Mr

Hoggett here, is tied right into the energy field contained in this meteorite.' The Doctor stared at the glossy black ball, and Amy could tell, even though he was made of stone, that his fantastic mind was already coming up with a plan. 'It's my guess that the molecular reconfiguration is controlled by a similar field.'

'What do you mean?'

'I've been thinking about Athrocite and his ability to turn things into moon stone. Do you remember I said that the transformation was unstable, and therefore reversible?' The Doctor paced quickly around the kitchen. 'Well, that's true – but only up to a point. Because once enough Earth matter has been converted, then it will reach a tipping point.'

'Which means?'

The Doctor stopped. 'Which means that the transformation will start to spread faster and faster. And it will be unstoppable. And it will not be possible to reverse it.'

'The point of no return,' realised Chris.

'But that means it could take over . . . everywhere,'

said Amy. 'And everything.'

'We have to stop it,' said the Doctor. 'And this meteorite is the key. We have to keep it away from Athrocite – as far away as possible.'

'But he'll follow it anywhere,' said Chris. 'He followed it all the way from the research centre to here.'

'I was thinking of taking it somewhat further away than that,' said the Doctor. He turned to Amy. 'Stay here with Chris and Jess – make sure no harm comes to Mr Conway or Mr Hoggett. And whatever you do, don't let Athrocite back in.'

Jess gaped at him, trying to imagine keeping the huge Rock Man from entering the farmhouse. 'What? How?'

'I don't know – you'll think of something.' The Doctor turned to Rory. 'Rory, I'm going to need your help. I can't move all that fast, so you'll have to take the meteorite.' He gave it to Rory. 'We'll go as a pair. On the count of three . . .'

'Hold on,' said Rory quickly. 'What are you talking about?'

'We need to get that meteorite on-board the TARDIS,' explained the Doctor, already heading for the door. 'And that means we've got to get past Athrocite first. Come on – there's not a second to lose!'

CHAPTER 29

TO THE TARDIS

They crept out into the farmyard, keeping low so that Athrocite couldn't easily spot them.

The Rock Man was still standing at the top end of the yard, surrounded by moon stone. He was deliberately touching more and more things – the barn, the engine shed, a tree – and transforming them into lunar rock.

'What's he doing?' whispered Rory.

'Turning everything he can get his hands on into moon rock,' replied the Doctor, as quietly as he could manage with his rasping rock-voice. 'He's trying to change everything – to reach the tipping point. Soon the effect will be unstoppable.'

'We'd best get a move on then.' Rory crept out from behind the Land Rover and motioned for the

Doctor to follow him.

Together they moved slowly up the farmyard, towards the TARDIS.

But that also took them nearer to Athrocite.

'Hopefully he's too busy trying to create a new world to notice us,' said the Doctor as they paused by the edge of the barn.

They moved on, darting from cover to cover.

But then disaster struck.

The Doctor's stone foot hit the edge of a pile of logs balanced against the side of the shed. Athrocite had already turned the logs into moon stone – but they were still loose. The Doctor's boot dislodged one of the lowermost logs – and the rest came tumbling down with a loud clatter.

Athrocite lumbered around, alerted by the noise.

But that wasn't all. The Doctor's legs had got caught up in the rock fall and he sprawled his length on the ground. For a hearts-stopping moment he thought he was going to be smashed to pieces.

'Doctor!' Rory skidded to a halt, eyes wide. He watched Athrocite start towards the fallen Doctor.

Rory panicked, thinking the Doctor must surely have cracked.

But the Doctor, miraculously, had landed in a large patch of mud. He slithered to a stop and tried to get up, but it was impossible to get a grip on the slippery ground.

Athrocite stalked towards him with a triumphant growl.

'Go!' the Doctor shouted at Rory.

Athrocite turned to see Rory on the other side of the yard.

The distraction was just enough for the Doctor. He crawled through the mud and dragged himself carefully up, using the wall of the barn for support.

Rory looked uncertainly at the Doctor, and then at the Rock Man.

And ran.

Athrocite roared and turned back to face the Doctor. He growled again as the stone figure walked calmly towards him.

'There's no point in getting all cross about it,' said the Doctor. 'You had your chance.'

Athrocite roared, flailing at him with a craggy arm. If the blow had connected, the Doctor would have been smashed to smithereens – but he dodged just in time.

Athrocite swung again, and the Doctor darted out of the way once more.

'You'll have to be faster than that,' the Doctor told him. He ducked another blow. 'I used to spar with Mohammed Ali – the greatest boxer who ever lived.'

The Rock Man lunged desperately, almost losing his footing in the mud. The Doctor skipped lightly under the blow – although it was a close thing. A piece of hair was chipped right off his head.

But Athrocite stumbled past, and the Doctor was free to run – or rather lumber – as quickly as his heavy stone legs would allow.

Rory had already reached the TARDIS. 'Doctor, hurry up!'

The Doctor trudged on up the hill. The TARDIS windows shone brightly, beckoning him forwards.

Behind him, Athrocite was pounding in pursuit.

The Doctor could hear the Rock Man's rasping growls growing closer. He wasn't as nimble as the Doctor, but he had longer legs and a bigger stride.

The Doctor pushed on wearily. He could feel the weight of every stone organ in his body.

Athrocite marched untiringly after him, threatening him with every kind of fate. Any hope of negotiating a peaceful settlement had gone. Sadly, the Doctor had to accept that it was now a case of simple survival.

He reached the pigsties. Percy the pregnant pig snuffled her way around the pen, searching in the muck and straw for anything good to eat. The other pigs squealed in shock and distress as the Doctor clambered over the fence.

He staggered across to the TARDIS and fell heavily against the wooden doors.

'Hurry, Doctor,' Rory yelled. 'He's gaining on us!'

Athrocite had reached the pigsty. His dark eyes blazed with fury and the pen was suddenly turned to moon stone. The grey rock spread across the concrete floor, the straw, the trough . . . and with a series of cracks and muffled grunts the pigs were turned to stone.

Percy gave an anguished squeal as her pink hide turned grey, then stiff and then solid.

The Doctor looked in dismay at the TARDIS key. 'It's turned to moon rock as well!'

He held up the key for Rory to see. The brass had been turned into a sliver of stone.

'Will it still work?' Rory asked.

'Let's see!' The Doctor carefully inserted the stone key into the lock on the police box door.

Athrocite clambered into the stone pigsty with a growl.

'Can't let him turn the TARDIS into moon rock!' said the Doctor, turning the key as gently as he could. He didn't want to snap it accidentally.

The police box door opened and the Doctor and Rory piled quickly inside.

CHAPTER 30
A RETURN TO NORMAL

Rory banged the TARDIS door shut behind them as the Doctor raced up the steps to the control console.

'Careful you don't fall!' Rory called after him.

'Got to be quick, Rory!' The Doctor ground to a halt at the console and began pulling levers and twisting dials at a frantic pace.

Rory was climbing up the stairs to the console deck just as the Doctor threw the dematerialisation lever. The TARDIS engines began to grind and groan and the strange glass elements inside the central column heaved up and down.

Outside, the blue police box faded from the pigsty with a harsh wheeze.

Athrocite roared, swiping at the air where the

TARDIS had stood. Then, with an angry grumble, he turned and stomped back down the hill towards the farmhouse.

The TARDIS lurched and spun, sparks flying from the circuits arranged around the complicated hexagonal console. Rory grabbed hold of the seat on the edge of the deck for support. 'Where are we going?'

'Away from here,' replied the Doctor, busy at the controls. Puffs of steam erupted from the console. The monitor screen suspended from its iron framework filled with complicated numbers and patterns.

Rory knew the TARDIS was in flight – hurtling helter-skelter through the mysterious region of space-time known only as the Vortex.

'We don't need to go too far,' said the Doctor, moving rapidly from one section of the console to another. He turned wheels, pumped handles and flicked switches with incredible speed for someone made of stone.

It always amazed Rory that the Doctor knew what any of the complex instruments actually did. The TARDIS was supposed to be a time machine, the product of a fantastically advanced civilisation that no longer existed – but most of the controls appeared to be made up of old bits of junk: taps, typewriters, cogs and other arcane pieces of machinery collected from across the universe and throughout history.

Like the Doctor, the TARDIS was something of a mystery.

The ancient engines began to wheeze and groan once more.

'Coming into land!' the Doctor declared loudly, as the old ship rattled to a stop.

The glass bubbles in the rotor column slowed to a halt and steam drifted from the depths of the TARDIS console.

'Doctor,' said Rory suddenly. 'Look at you . . .'

The Doctor twisted a shaving mirror around so that he could see his face. The greyness of the moon stone was beginning to fade. His skin was looking pinker, fleshier and his hair was loosening and turning dark once more.

'You're turning back to normal!' Rory said with relief.

'We're far enough away from Athrocite for the molecular transformation to start unravelling,' said the Doctor. He sounded very relieved himself. 'I wonder what's happening back on the farm?'

Jess and Amy peered out of the kitchen window and gasped in shock.

Outside, there was little more than a lunar landscape.

The entire farm had been turned into moon stone. The land beyond was turning greyer, dustier and more lifeless as they watched.

'When is it going to end?' wondered Jess.

Athrocite was now walking towards the farmhouse. His heavy tread shook the ground as he approached the door.

'He's going to turn us to stone now,' Jess realised.

'Not if I can help it,' said Chris. He picked up a

kitchen chair. 'The Doctor said we mustn't let him back into the farmhouse. We may have to fight.'

'Don't be daft,' said Jess miserably. 'How can we hold off a thing like that?'

'We have to try,' Amy said.

Athrocite loomed in the doorway. The black holes of his eyes bored pitilessly into the farmhouse, looking for the human beings cowering inside.

'To think I almost felt sorry for him,' said Amy. Her heart was banging away inside her chest, full of fear. She knew that Jess was probably right – there was no way they could stop the Rock Man now.

'I'll fight if I have to,' Chris said, raising the chair, as he stepped bravely towards the creature.

'And I'll fight with you,' said Ralph Conway.

The farmer stepped up alongside Chris. He was completely back to normal – full of his original health and colour, with not a shred of moon stone about him apart from a thin layer of lunar dust. In his hand he gripped a stout wooden stick.

'Dad!' cried Jess in sheer delight. She put a hand to her mouth as tears of happiness sprang into her eyes.

Mr Hogget had also been restored. 'What the–'

But Ralph Conway turned and pointed at Hoggett and said, very firmly, 'Not. One. More. Word.'

And Mr Hoggett fell silent.

'The Doctor did it!' Jess said. She gave Amy a hug. 'He did it!'

'It's not over yet,' warned Amy.

Athrocite snarled in the doorway, advancing another step towards Chris and Ralph. The humans looked puny and soft in his presence.

'Keep back,' ordered Chris.

There was a moment's pause – and then Athrocite roared and attacked.

CHAPTER 31
THE ACTUAL MOON

Rory stood in the open doorway of the TARDIS and blinked.

'We're on the moon,' he said. 'The actual moon.'

'The actual moon,' confirmed the Doctor, joining him.

The Doctor was completely restored – full of health and vigour, tugging his bow tie carefully back into shape. His tweed jacket looked none the worse for wear – although there were a couple of small scratches visible on the Doctor's face and hands.

There was a plaster on the tip of one of his fingers too. 'Chipped a fragment off when I fell in the yard,' he explained to Rory.

Rory was still staring at the airless grey landscape outside. For as far as he could see, there was nothing but grey dust and craters. The surface of the moon.

The sky was utterly black, but dotted with stars and one large, cloudy blue sphere: Earth.

'Wow,' Rory said. He'd been to fifteenth century Venice, met many kinds of alien and seen all sorts of wonders with the Doctor. But there was something special about this. Perhaps it was because it was just him and the Doctor alone. It was a private viewing of his own planet's only natural satellite.

'Can we go out?' Rory asked. 'One small step for man, one giant leap for Rory Williams?'

The Doctor smiled but shook his head. 'Best not. The force field is keeping the air inside the TARDIS. Step out there and it's nothing but a cold, airless vacuum. You'd need a spacesuit.'

'You must have spacesuits on the TARDIS.'

'But not enough time.' The Doctor patted Rory on the shoulder. 'I know that sounds a bit ironic, with this being a time machine and everything, but we ought to get on with what we came here for.'

Rory looked down at the meteorite in his hand. The strange alien ball from the dawn of the universe that had landed on the moon nearly four billion years ago. The tiny meteorite that had been found by the *Apollo* astronauts and brought back to Earth for study. The meteorite that had caused all the trouble in the first place.

'Back where it belongs,' Rory said, and hurled the ball far out onto the surface of the moon. It bounced a couple of times, lazily in the lighter gravity, and then settled in a dust mound.

'It doesn't really belong anywhere,' said the Doctor. 'But it will be safe up here.'

Rory took one last look out of the police box. 'Wow,' he said again.

Back on Earth, in the Conway farmhouse, Athrocite roared in anger.

And then roared in pain.

He stiffened, shot through with a terrible agony. The sound that emerged from his stone lips was one that Amy would have nightmares about for a long time afterwards: a strange, awful cry, like the noise of rocks breaking but slowed down into one long, agonisingly drawn-out crack.

Splits in the surface of the Rock Man's body spread like roadways across a map, weaving in and out of the lumps and bumps of his craggy skin. Dust poured from the cracks as they widened and extended.

'Omigosh, what's happening to him?' Jess wondered, appalled.

They all stepped back sharply as the Rock Man crumbled in front of them.

The splits joined together in a sudden, massive, breakdown. The creature broke up into pieces, chunks falling away as he stumbled forward.

The giant head split from the body and then that too crumbled into fragments.

Before long, there was nothing more than a pile of broken rock and dust on the floor.

Completely inanimate.

Dead.

A breeze lifted the dust away in a grey cloud and a loud wheezing and groaning noise filled the farmhouse.

A second later, a large blue police box materialised in the middle of the kitchen.

The TARDIS door opened and the Doctor and Rory emerged. Amy ran over and clipped her husband lightly on the arm. 'Hey! You! Where've you been?'

Rory smiled at her. 'I've been to the moon, Amy!'

'Wow, yeah, great – been there, done that,' Amy said. Then she laughed and gave him a quick, embarrassed hug. 'Don't look so hurt. It's good to have you back, you big lump – I missed you.'

'And here's one big lump that we won't miss,' said the Doctor, poking the pile of rocks on the floor with the toe of his boot. 'All that remains of Athrocite, I presume?'

'He just went to pieces,' said Chris. 'Literally.'

'We threw the meteorite back where it came from,' explained the Doctor. He knelt down and rubbed some of the moon dust between his fingers. 'It reversed the molecular reconfiguration that Athrocite started – and not a moment too soon.'

'Everything's back to normal outside, too,' said Jess.

The farmyard and the surrounding countryside were back to their usual muddy state. The Land Rover, the tractor and the barn were all back. Even the farmyard wall that Ralph had struggled to repair the night before had been restored. There wasn't a trace of moon rock anywhere.

'But what about all this?' asked Mr Hoggett grumpily, indicating the pile of rubble on the floor. 'The remains of Athrocite – or whatever its name was.'

'Here, have a bit,' the Doctor chucked a piece of the moon rock to Hoggett. 'As a souvenir.'

'A souvenir?' Hoggett looked down at the small stone in his hand – and watched in surprise as it crumbled into dust and then faded from view.

The rest of the rock disappeared too.

'What happened to it?'

The Doctor shrugged. 'Athrocite was an artificial being in many ways – constructed out of nothing but moon dust by the meteorite. It's no surprise that he's returned to his original state.'

Mr Hoggett brushed his hands clean. 'Some souvenir! I might have known. It's high time I left, anyway – it looks like you've all got a lot of tidying up to do!'

CHAPTER 32
A WIN–WIN SITUATION

A little later, after they had helped tidy the place up yet again and enjoyed a long-overdue cup of tea, everyone stood by the TARDIS.

The Doctor had his key out – now back to its original shiny brass – and was eager to go. He hated long goodbyes.

'It's been . . . interesting,' Jess said with a smile. 'I'll be sorry to see you go.'

'But go we must,' said the Doctor. He unlocked the TARDIS door.

'Wait a second,' said Rory. 'What about Percy the pregnant pig? Is she OK?'

'She's fine,' Jess laughed. 'We should see a big litter of piglets any day soon.'

'And what about Chris?' asked Amy. 'How are you?'

'I'm fine too,' Chris said. He put an arm around Jess. 'No piglets on the way though. At least, not yet.'

'Don't be too long about it,' grumbled Ralph Conway. 'We could do with plenty more help around here.'

'I've agreed to come and live on the farm,' Chris explained with a smile. 'Do some real work for a change.'

'He's more than welcome,' Ralph said. 'So long as he pulls his weight with the chores.'

'What about your work at the research centre?' asked the Doctor. 'Won't they mind?'

'I've been in touch with them,' Chris said. 'They're too busy trying to work out what went wrong and why their top secret lab has been reduced to a mangled heap of spare parts.'

'Ah – awkward questions,' nodded the Doctor, as if he was more than familiar with those. 'Best keep out of it.'

'I intend to.'

'And what about Mr Hoggett?' asked Rory.

'He's offered to pay for a lot of the rebuilding

work on the farm,' said Jess. 'It came as a bit of a surprise – but apparently he's willing to pay anything so long as he never has to come here or see any of us again.'

'Sounds like a win-win situation,' Rory laughed.

'And they're just the kind I like,' said the Doctor.

They said their goodbyes and then disappeared inside the TARDIS. Moments later, Jess, Chris and Ralph watched as the police box faded from sight.

The Doctor, Amy and Rory were on their way again – to amazing new adventures.

The End

DOCTOR ⬡ WHO

DEATH RIDERS

Justin Richards

The Galactic Fair has arrived on the mining asteroid of Stanalan and anticipation is building around the construction of the fair's most popular attraction – the Death Ride! But there is something sinister going on behind all the fun of the fair; people are mysteriously dying in the Off-Limits tunnels. Join the Doctor, Amy and Rory as they investigate…

Also available:

The Good the Bad and the Alien
by Colin Brake

System Wipe by Oli Smith

Coming soon:

Rain of Terror by Mike Tucker

Extra Time by Richard Dungworth

The Underwater War by Richard Dinnick

Terminal of Despair by Steve Lyons

DOCTOR WHO

DEATH RIDERS

Justin Richards

Cover illustrated by Paul Campbell

BBC Children's Books
Published by the Penguin Group
Penguin Books Ltd, 80 Strand, London, WC2R 0RL, England
Penguin Group (USA) Inc., 375 Hudson Street, New York 10014, USA
Penguin Books (Australia) Ltd, 250 Camberwell Road, Camberwell,
Victoria 3124, Australia (A division of Pearson Australia Group PTY Ltd)
Penguin Group (NZ), 67 Apollo Drive, Rosedale, North Shore
0632, New Zealand (A division of Pearson New Zealand Ltd)
Canada, India, South Africa
Published by BBC Children's Books, 2011
Text and design © Children's Character Books
Heart of Stone written by Trevor Baxendale
Death Riders written by Justin Richards
Covers illustrated by Paul Campbell

2

ISBN – 978-14059-0-757-6

Mixed Sources
Product group from well-managed
forests and other controlled sources
www.fsc.org Cert no. SA-COC-1592
© 1996 Forest Stewardship Council

Printed in Great Britain by Clays Ltd, St Ives plc

CONTENTS

CHAPTER 1
SHORT CUT TO DEATH

The rock walls were damp and slippery. The only light came from Rodge's torch. He made his way carefully along the tunnel, avoiding the deeper puddles where the water had pooled after running down the walls. It was condensation from the difference in temperature – the warm, processed air meeting the cold rock of the asteroid's interior.

Rodge had lost track of how long he'd been walking. But he had to reach one of the main tunnels soon. In his mental map of the tunnel system, this should have been a short cut. But it wasn't working out that way. He paused and looked back, trying to see if the tunnel sloped. It didn't seem to, but over the distance he must have come even a slight incline would mean he missed the main tunnel. He could be above or below it. Maybe he'd do better to head back the way he'd come and take one of the proper routes.

Or maybe, if he kept going, in just a few metres he'd be able to see the light from the main tunnel. Maybe he'd soon be laughing at how he'd thought he was lost, and how he'd got scared sneaking through one of the Off-Limits.

Scared . . . Was he scared? No, of course he wasn't. In the worst case, he would simply retrace his steps back to Blue 17 and then take the long route. He'd be late and Korl, his supervisor, would shout at him. They were all waiting for the survey results Rodge was carrying.

Rodge paused, listening to try to hear the sound of machinery. If he could hear the robot drills or rock-luggers he'd know he was close to the workings. But the only sound he could hear was the steady drop-drip-drip of water. Like the beating of a heart, or the measured tread of someone walking towards him in the darkness.

He shivered at the thought and turned a full circle. His torchlight glistened on the damp, uneven walls and reflected off the shallow puddles. He'd better go back, he decided at last. He was just getting further and further away from where he was meant to be.

For a moment his stomach tensed. Which way had he come? He'd turned a full circle – or had he? Rodge took a deep breath of warm recycled air as he tried to think. He was sure it was that way – that was the direction he'd come from. Yes, of course – there was the jutting bit of rock near the tunnel floor that he'd grazed his leg on. Had to be.

He took a minute to allow his nerves to settle

before heading back. Bad move – he'd never take a short cut on his own again. At least, not one he didn't already know.

As he stood there, preparing to hurry back the way he'd come, Rodge frowned. He could hear something now, he was sure. Something other than the dripping water and his own ragged breathing. A scuffling sound. Something moving.

He turned quickly, holding the torch at arm's length so it illuminated as much as possible. But there was nothing. Just rock walls, damp reflections and the ever-present shadows.

One of the shadows detached itself from the others. Claws clicked and scraped on the hard floor. Something dark and shapeless hurled itself out of the darkness.

Rodge caught only a glimpse of the creature. Staring eyes wide with fury and hunger. Claws ripping through the air towards him. Teeth glinting in the frantic torchlight.

Then he dropped the torch. The light went out, leaving only the faintest pale glow from the tunnel walls.

The last thing Rodge thought as an even greater blackness wiped through his mind was that he could hear music. Mournful, sad music. Like a lament for the dead.

CHAPTER 2
INTO THE TUNNELS

The central column of the TARDIS thumped to a halt and the protesting, tortured rasping of the engines stopped.

'This is the exciting bit,' the Doctor announced. He grabbed his tweed jacket off the back of a chair and stuffed his arm down a sleeve. The jacket flapped as he tried to get the other arm into the other sleeve, and he ended up twisting round and round in a circle like a dog chasing its own tail.

Amy grabbed his collar and held the jacket so he could finish putting it on. 'You're hopeless,' she told him.

'Lucky I've got you then.'

'Lucky you've got us both,' she retorted.

'Absolutely.' The Doctor turned to Rory. 'Is my bow tie straight?'

'Not really,' Rory told him.

'Excellent!' the Doctor bounded down to the TARDIS doors. 'Come on then. Let's see what's outside.'

'Don't you know?' Rory asked as he and Amy followed.

'Where's the fun in knowing?'

The Doctor grasped the handle, ready to pull the door open.

'Just so long as it's safe,' Rory muttered.

The Doctor hesitated. 'That's a thought,' he said seriously. Then he grinned. 'No – just kidding. Of course it's safe. There's air and gravity and hardly any radiation. What more can you ask for?'

'Sunshine and flowers?' Amy said.

'Safety and beauty,' Rory suggested.

'Yeah, all those. But apart from that, what? I can promise you, whatever is out there will be thrilling and exciting. It'll be new and different. It will be… '

With a theatrical flourish, the Doctor pulled the door open.

'Damp and boring and made of rock,' Amy said.

On the other side of the TARDIS door was a rough wall of dark rock. A droplet of water ran down its glistening surface and dripped on to the Doctor's shoe. He watched it all the way.

'Obviously we're not going anywhere,' Rory said.

He reached out to close the door again, but the Doctor slapped his hand away. 'I think rock, dark damp rock, is new, different, thrilling and exciting,' he said grumpily.

Amy laughed. 'You would.'

'No, no, no – I do.'

The Doctor reached out, ran his finger down the damp wall and then licked it.

Rory grimaced. 'Oh, that's gross.'

The Doctor ignored him. 'Traces of trisilicate. This wall has been machine-cut – look, you can see the scratches and grooves where the robot cutting tools have sheared through it. The damp is condensation, which suggests the rock itself is cold, but the air is warm. The fact there is air, and gravity, means there's artificial life support plumbed into this asteroid, which means there are people here, too.'

'Show off,' Amy said.

'All of which is exciting and thrilling like I said, wouldn't you agree?' The Doctor tapped the tip of his damp finger on Amy's nose.

'I might,' she admitted. 'If we could get out of the door.'

'Easily fixed.'

The Doctor slammed the door shut and ran back to the control console.

'How do you know it's an asteroid?' Rory asked. 'Not that I'm really interested,' he added. 'Well, I'm a bit interested, which is why I asked. But only a bit. Not in the thrilled, excited sense of interested.'

'Good question,' the Doctor conceded.

The central column began to move slowly as the sound of the TARDIS engines echoed around.

'Composition of the rock is typical of an asteroid in the Mangall system,' the Doctor went on, adjusting a control, checking a dial and thumping a button. 'That would fit with the mining operations too, assuming this is the thirty-third century, which it is.'

The TARDIS engines ground to a halt again.

'And in any case, I checked the readings when we landed.'

'So you already knew?' Amy asked.

'I did.'

'Then why didn't you tell us?' Rory said.

'And deny you the chance to be thrilled and excited and . . . all that?'

'Could have lived with it,' Rory muttered.

The Doctor was back at the TARDIS door. 'Second time lucky.'

'So where are we now?' Amy wanted to know.

'Pretty much where we were before. I just turned us round.'

The Doctor pulled the door open. This time they could see a rocky tunnel stretching away into the distance. The Doctor led them outside and closed the door. He pointed to the tunnel wall next to the TARDIS.

'There you are – I licked that.' His expression turned into a frown and he inspected his finger. 'Why did I do that? It was gross. Rory – you said it was gross and you were right. Don't let me lick walls again, right? Not ever.'

Amy was looking round. The TARDIS was standing against the wall of a wide tunnel hewn from the dark, damp rock. The tunnel was about four metres high and roughly the same width.

'So, we're in a mining tunnel dug by some sort of robot drilling machine deep inside an asteroid in the whatever system you said it was, right?' Amy said.

'Right.'

'So how come we can see? Where is the light coming from?' She pointed at the roof. 'No lights – look. But there's light from somewhere.'

'It's as if the walls are sort of glowing,' Rory said. 'Except they're not.'

'Fluripsent crystals,' the Doctor said. 'Clever, eh?'

'Floor-what?'

'The mining drills embed them in the walls when they dig them out. They emit a radiant light. Which means the walls glow – only they don't.

Good description, Rory. It's a bit like throwing your voice, you know, how a ventriloquist does. Only the crystals throw light, so it seems to come from somewhere else.'

'It seems to come from all round us,' Amy said.

'Like I told you. It's clever. Now, let's go and see if we can find someone to tell us exactly where we are.'

'How do you know there's anyone here?' Rory asked. 'You talked about robot drills and stuff. Maybe there are no people.'

'There's air,' Amy pointed out.

'Might need that for the robots,' Rory said. 'OK, before you say it, I know robots don't breathe. But car engines need air for internal combustion, don't they?'

'Good points, both of you,' the Doctor said. 'But robots don't need light. Not these sorts of robots anyway. And the crystals are expensive. They'll only embed them in tunnels that people use, and use regularly. Anywhere else, you need a torch.'

'So which way do we go?' Amy asked.

'Towards the noise,' Rory said.

As they had been talking, a low rumbling sound was building in volume. It was getting louder all the time and the ground beneath their feet was beginning to vibrate.

'This way.' The Doctor set off briskly down the tunnel. After several steps, he stopped abruptly, swung round and headed in the opposite direction. 'This way. Definitely this way.'

They hadn't been able to see from further back that another tunnel cut across the one where the TARDIS had landed. An enormous vehicle appeared, as if out of the tunnel wall, and lumbered slowly over the crossroads and off down the other tunnel. It was like a massive bulldozer, on caterpillar tracks, but with a huge conical drill on the front. It was dusty and dented, obviously very old. There didn't seem to be any exhaust, but Amy could detect an oily smell in the air as the sound died away.

'Do we follow it?' Rory asked as they reached the crossroads.

The Doctor shook his head. 'We're looking for people, not the drill face. It's off to do some mining. That's boring machine work.' He grinned. 'And I do really mean boring.'

As the sound of the mining machine faded, Amy could hear another sound in the distance. It was very faint but it was coming from further down the tunnel they were in.

'What's that?' she asked, puzzled. 'I mean – it sounds like . . .'

'It sounds like an electric organ,' Rory said. 'But, I mean, it can't be. Can it?'

'One way to find out,' the Doctor told them. 'And that way is onwards.' He strode off along the tunnel towards the sound.

Ahead of them, Amy could see that the

tunnel opened out into a vast cavern. The size of the chamber was truly stunning. But that wasn't what made her gape in astonishment.

'What?!' Rory gasped.

'I don't believe it,' Amy said.

The sound of the electronic organ was louder now. As they got nearer they could hear people laughing and talking. They could smell the food that was being cooked. They could also hear other, quieter music . . .

'Well, there's something you don't see every day in a vast cavern deep inside an asteroid floating in space,' the Doctor said.

Small tents and side stalls were arranged around the edge of the cavern. Larger tents were clustered in the middle. A white-faced clown on stilts walked past, waving to a child who was eating candyfloss. A small crowd of people gasped in unison as a fire-eater spat flames into the air. Wooden horses rose and fell as they went round a large carousel.

They were looking at a huge fairground.

CHAPTER 3
FUN AT THE FAIR

Somehow the Doctor had acquired a large stick of yellow candyfloss. And a toffee apple. The candyfloss stuck to his chin so it looked like he had a wispy yellow beard. Amy tried not to laugh. And failed.

'What?' the Doctor asked, laughing too. 'Oh.' Realising, he wiped his chin with his other hand – leaving streaks of sugary toffee down his cheek from the apple he was holding. 'Better?'

Amy bit back her laughter. 'Much.'

They spent a while just wandering around looking at the various stalls and sideshows. There was a hoopla and a large plastic pool where you had to hook plastic toy animals that looked a bit like ducks (but weren't) out of the water. If your not-a-duck had a black cross on the bottom, then you won a prize. Rory didn't.

There were jugglers and acrobats performing in a roped off area. In the middle of the cavern – further away from the glowing walls that didn't glow – globes of light hung in the air. The tents offered fortune-telling, speeches from famous plays, and tea and cake.

The electric organ music turned out to be coming from the carousel. The wooden (if they were indeed wooden) horses (if indeed they were horses) performed tirelessly for children (who really were children) in simple overalls and smocks. Everyone was dusty and grimy. But everyone was happy and laughing. Everyone was having the time of their lives.

Everyone except, judging by his expression, Rory.

'Oh, what's wrong?' Amy challenged him. She grabbed Rory's arm and snuggled her cheek against his shoulder.

'I didn't win on the hook-a-not-a-duck,' he grumbled.

'You're sulking about that?' Amy was surprised. 'But the prize was a bouncy ball. It was rubbish.'

'Still didn't win,' Rory complained. But he was trying not to smile now. 'I could have thrown the prize away. And it would have bounced.'

The Doctor was looking up at the white-faced clown on stilts. 'What's your name?' he called. 'Happy?'

'No,' the clown told him, his white face expressionless. 'They call me Clueless.'

'Clueless the Clown,' Amy said. 'I like it.'

'So why do they call you that?' Rory asked.

The clown shrugged. 'I haven't a clue.'

The Doctor laughed. Amy and Rory laughed too, as the clown lumbered away on his stilts.

'Should have seen that one coming,' Rory admitted.

'You walked right into it,' Amy agreed. 'On stilts. Hey, look – is that a coconut shy?'

'We're supposed to be finding out where we are,' the Doctor reminded her.

'Oh, I love coconuts,' Rory said.

'You find out where we are,' Amy told the Doctor. 'Rory and me are going to win a coconut, isn't that right?'

'That's right,' Rory agreed.

'No, it isn't,' the Doctor protested. 'It's not even close. "Rory and me are going to win a coconut"? How can you even say that?'

'Sorry,' Amy said, unsure quite what the problem was.

'It's "Rory and I",' the Doctor corrected her. 'It's "Rory and I are going to win a coconut."'

'Are we?' Rory asked the Doctor.

'No,' Amy told the Doctor. 'You are going to

find out where we are. Rory and me are going to win a coconut.'

The Doctor looked at her for a moment. His eyes narrowed slightly. He opened his mouth to say something, then closed it again. Finally he nodded. 'Fair enough,' he said. 'I'll meet you back here in half an hour.'

To Amy's delight and Rory's obvious surprise, they won a coconut. Amy managed to hit one of the coconuts, but just knocked it sideways a bit.

'At least you can tell they're not glued down,' Rory told her.

'It's better than you've done,' Amy pointed out.

So Rory bought another set of three balls to throw, using some of the coins the Doctor had just happened to have with him that seemed to work here. His first shot hit the same coconut, and sent it flying out of its stand.

'Result!' Amy exclaimed.

The man running the stall was large and hairy with rolled-up sleeves revealing arms covered with tattoos. But his grizzled face broke into a broken-toothed grin as he retrieved the coconut for Rory and set another one in its place.

'Well done, lad,' he said.

Feeling his luck must be on the turn, Rory had another go at hooking a not-a-duck. But with as little success as the first time. They still had ten minutes to wait for the Doctor, so Amy suggested they find somewhere that was selling hot drinks. They both recalled seeing a tent serving tea and cake, but neither of them could remember exactly where it was.

It took them almost the whole ten minutes to get back to where they'd seen the tent.

'He'll be late,' Amy said. 'Let's get tea anyway.'

'Or we could wait, in case he isn't late,' Rory suggested.

'He's always late,' Amy said.

'Who is?' the Doctor asked, arriving beside them.

'Nothing,' Amy said quickly, glaring at Rory to keep him quiet. 'So,' she went on, 'what have you found out?'

'Lots.' The Doctor grinned, evidently pleased with himself. 'Lots and lots. Did you win a – ' He broke off, as Rory held out his coconut, grin freezing. 'Ah.'

'That surprised you, didn't it?' Rory asked him.

'Er, well, yes it did. I have to admit I am surprised. You think that's a coconut, don't you?'

'It is a coconut,' Amy said.

'Course it is.' The Doctor nodded, just too enthusiastically. 'A coconut. Just don't eat it, that's all. Or break it open. Whatever you do, don't break it open.'

'Why not?' Amy asked.

Rory was examining the coconut cautiously, weighing it in his hand. 'What's the problem?'

'Well, I could be wrong,' the Doctor admitted, 'but that does look suspiciously like the egg of a wilderbird from Deuteronomy Nine. Nasty things, wilderbirds. They're like birds. Only, um, wilder. If you feel it sort of vibrating, put it down ever so carefully and then run like hell.'

Rory held the 'coconut' at arm's length. 'You are kidding me.'

The Doctor gently lifted the coconut from Rory's palm. He tossed it high in the air and caught it again. 'Yes,' he said. 'I'm kidding you. It's a coconut.' He handed it back to a relieved Rory. 'Well, probably,' he added. 'Anyone fancy a cuppa? I'm parched and they do cake as well.'

Over tea and cake – which was green with purple bits in it – the Doctor explained what he had learned from chatting to some of the fairground visitors and stall holders.

'We're on a mining asteroid called Stanalan,'

he said, through a mouthful of green-bitty cake. 'Sorry, did that get you?' He brushed damp crumbs off Amy's shoulder. 'Like I thought, it's in the Torajii system.'

'That's not what you said,' Amy told him.

The Doctor ignored her. 'Automated mining mostly, and most of the original miners have stayed on and become colonists. Obviously they still have to do some digging by hand as well as maintaining the equipment and doing the paperwork. Robots never do admin, which is a shame as that would really be a help.'

'So these people actually live down here?' Rory asked.

The Doctor nodded, then took a slurp of tea. 'Quite a little community. There's a hospital, a school, little shops and even a local orchestra. Well, I guess there's not a lot to do in the damp, dark underground – they live in worked-out tunnels. So they're pretty chuffed that the

Galactic Fair has come to town.'

'I can imagine,' Amy said.

A large grey-haired woman in a dark uniform with a white pinafore dress busied herself clearing away Amy and Rory's tea things. The Doctor lifted his cup so she could wipe the table underneath.

'As well as Mad Milly the Fortune-Teller,' he said, 'there's Clueless the Clown, carousels, candyfloss, coconuts and lots of other things beginning with the letter 'C'. And someone called Garvo and his Dancing Drexxon, whatever that is . . . Oh yes, they've got it all. We arrived at just the right time.'

'And tea,' the woman wiping the table pointed out. 'Best tea in the sector.'

The Doctor raised his cup in salute. 'Best tea in the galaxy,' he assured her. 'Believe me, I know about tea. And galaxies.'

'And tomorrow,' the woman added, 'they

should have the Death Ride finished.'

'Death Ride?' Rory asked, his eyes widening slightly.

'I think we've probably been closer to death than a fairground ride will take us,' Amy told him.

The woman laughed. 'Don't you believe it.' She shook her head in the manner of someone who knows something that everyone else can't even begin to suspect. Then she hurried away. Still laughing.

'That's encouraging,' Amy said brightly.

'Don't think I fancy a Death Ride,' Rory decided.

The Doctor was watching the woman as she cleared another table. 'Death Ride,' he said, enjoying the words and rolling them round his mouth. 'I am going to have to try that!'

Amy and Rory agreed that they would find out more about the Death Ride, and maybe even take a look at it. They did not agree, despite the

Doctor's enthusiastic pleas, to have a go. Not before they knew more.

'Fair play,' the Doctor decided eventually. 'But I bet when you see it, you'll love it.'

As they left the tea tent, Amy stopped. She could hear music. It wasn't the harsh tones of the electric organ music that accompanied the merry-go-round. It was a haunting tune. The notes lingered sadly. The melody seemed to drift through the cavern from all directions.

'Listen – where's it coming from?' Amy wondered.

The Doctor licked his finger and held it up as if testing the air. 'This way,' he decided.

'Or that way,' Rory suggested.

But Amy was already heading in a different direction from either of their suggestions. Sure enough, the music grew louder. She could see a little crowd of people gathered round one of the smaller tents. Unlike the other audiences, who cheered and laughed and talked and booed good-naturedly, these people were completely silent. Enthralled by the music.

The people at the back of the group were drifting away, having seen and heard enough. They nodded to each other, murmuring in quiet admiration.

Amy found herself moving to the front of the crowd as the music came to a melancholy end. The two people in front of her moved aside. Amy pushed through to see what was attracting all the attention, what was making the unique, haunting music.

A furry mass of claws and teeth reared up. Amy gasped in surprise and fear as the creature hissed angrily, its yellow eyes fixed unerringly on her.

CHAPTER 4
DANCE OF THE DREXXON

The snarl of the creature turned into something that sounded more like giggling. Rather than rearing up to attack, Amy realised it was hopping from one furry foot to the other – dancing a sort of jig.

The music came from a mouth organ played by a young man standing a short way behind the furry creature. A leash was tied round the man's wrist, the other end attached to the furry animal's own thin wrist. The young man's features were pale, contrasting with his coal-black hair. His clothes were tattered and frayed, old and grubby. His appearance seemed to suit the sad tune he was playing.

And the creature – which was only about a metre tall and covered in reddish-brown fur – hopped and danced to the rhythm and the mood of the man's playing.

'Raggedy musician,' the Doctor murmured in Amy's ear. 'And his performing . . . thing.'

'What is it?' Rory asked, squeezing through the crowd to join them. 'The thing?'

'Dunno,' the Doctor admitted. 'Not a monkey, though there's some similarity. Not seen one of those before.'

The music warbled to an end. The dancing furry creature that looked a bit like a monkey, but wasn't, stopped dancing. Its eyes scanned the people as some of them dropped coins into a carefully placed bucket and others just moved away. The man lowered his mouth organ. For a moment his face was a blank mask, as if he was still caught up in the other-world of his music. Then he switched on a smile and bowed theatrically.

'Thank you, thank you.' The man picked up the bucket and shook it, making the coins inside jingle and jangle. He held it out and a few more people dropped coins into it.

'Paying for slavery,' Amy said, backing away.

'You what?' Rory asked.

'That poor thing, whatever it is. Look – he has to keep it on a lead to stop it escaping. It's like performing apes or bears. It shouldn't be allowed.'

Rory shrugged. 'Can't see the problem. The thing seems happy enough, and well fed. It's not like the guy's stuck a ring through its nose or chains round its legs. How's it different from taking a dog for a walk?'

'Making it perform. It's shameful. Probably trained it on hot coals or something. What do you think Doc–'

But the Doctor was no longer standing beside

them. Amy looked round, and saw that he was talking excitedly to the musician.

'I saw your face,' the musician said as Amy strode up to him. 'I'm sorry if my Drexxon frightened you.' The furry creature snuggled against the man's leg, and he bent to ruffle its fur affectionately.

'Frightened?' Amy said, pursing her lips and shaking her head. 'I wasn't frightened. Just . . . a bit startled.' She turned to Rory for support – in time to see him pointing at her and mouthing, 'Frightened.'

'Sorry,' Rory said quickly.

'All friends now,' the Doctor announced, clapping his hands together. 'This is Garvo.' He pointed to the musician. 'And this Drexxon you've already met, when he didn't frighten you, not even a teensy-weensy bit. I don't think he has a name as such, so just call him Drexxon.'

'Hi,' Amy said, forcing a smile.

The Drexxon made the giggling noise again, sharp little teeth clacking together. It wrapped its warm furry arms round Amy's legs and purred like a cat.

'So, if we're all friends having such a jolly time –' Amy began.

'Here we go,' Rory murmured, shuffling in embarrassment.

'How come,' Amy went on, 'your little friend here is on a lead?'

If Garvo was surprised or put out by the question, he didn't show it. His expression didn't change from the fixed smile. 'It's not to keep him from running off or anything, and it's not uncomfortable. It's a link between us. It . . . helps.' He shrugged as if unsure what else to say.

'Helps? How can tying him to you help?'

'Well, I'm tied to him as well. We perform as a team. More than that – he feels the music I play on my harmonica.' He showed them the mouth organ. 'And I play music that responds to his reaction to it. The lead is like the musical link between us. As I said, it helps. It helps me to judge how he's dancing, from the way the lead moves while I'm playing. I can't always see exactly what he's up to, or predict what he'll do next. But I get signals, clues along the lead.'

'And can Drexxon here feel your music the same way?' the Doctor asked. He paused to kneel down and tickle the creature. 'Along the lead?'

'He can,' Garvo said. 'Obviously he can't talk, but he seems to be able to tell what notes are coming, the rhythm, from the way my hand moves while playing. He can feel that down the lead. We've been together for a long time. And he's a very sensitive little soul.'

'So I see,' Rory commented.

Drexxon was lying on his back now and letting the Doctor tickle his tummy.

'You have a go, Amy,' the Doctor suggested.

'Go on – he won't bite. Probably.'

Certainly the creature seemed happy enough, Amy thought. Although probably the only way to be sure would be to take him off the lead and see if he ran off. She rubbed her hand over Drexxon's warm tummy and was rewarded with more of the purring and giggling.

'Happy now?' Rory asked as Amy straightened up again.

'I was wrong,' she admitted. 'You happy now?'

'Wrong?' Rory echoed in mock surprise.

'OK, I was wrong about the lead and I was wrong to be frightened of him. A bit frightened of him. More startled than frightened, in fact. But I've tickled his tummy now, so I know that Drexxon is really a pussycat. All right?'

Rory frowned. 'Really?' He leaned closer, talking quietly. 'A pussycat? You mean, like dressed up – in a costume or something?'

Amy stared at him. 'Not a real pussycat, you

dozy. He's a space-monkey creature-thing. I mean, he's quiet and tame and friendly. Like a pussycat.'

Rory nodded slowly. 'I knew that.'

'Course you did.'

Something had changed at the fair. It took Amy a few moments to work out what it was.

'Why's everything suddenly so quiet?' she whispered to the Doctor.

'Search me,' he whispered back. 'Well, not literally search me, obviously.' He buttoned his jacket, as if to make sure she didn't actually search him.

'Everyone's heading that way,' Rory pointed out.

The people were all moving towards one side of the vast cavern. They were no longer laughing and talking excitedly, but looked sad and were moving slowly.

'What's going on?' Rory asked Garvo. 'New

shift starting or something?'

Garvo sighed. Even Drexxon looked a little downcast. 'It's time for the procession. A sad time. I'll stay here, and keep Drexxon out of the way. But most of the fair people will attend, as a mark of respect. You should go.'

'Yes, we should,' the Doctor told him. 'Come on,' he said to Amy and Rory.

'But what's going on, what's it all about?' Amy asked.

'No idea. But whatever it is, we should show respect – I got that much.'

They followed the last few people past the silent stalls and attractions. The merry-go-round horses stood still, silent and glassy-eyed. On the other side of the crowd, more music started. It was as sad as Garvo's harmonica, but bigger and bolder – played by a whole orchestra.

The Doctor found them a spot on the small stage used by the jugglers. From here they could see over the heads of most of the people. The orchestra was made up of about thirty people – each wearing a plain black tabard over the top of their everyday overalls. There were violins, trumpets and several brass instruments that Amy didn't recognise. At the back of the orchestra was a small floating platform that carried a harpist, a keyboard player and a drummer. Amy was surprised how many of the musicians were children. A small man dressed entirely in black conducted them, his face a mask of sadness.

Behind the orchestra four more men, all standing tall and proud but as sad-faced as the conductor, walked slowly and stiffly out of a wide tunnel and into the cavern. It took Amy a few moments to see that they were carrying something on their shoulders.

It took her a few moments more to realise that it was a coffin.

The pall-bearers carried the coffin past

the orchestra and the assembled crowd, and into another, narrower tunnel. The orchestra continued to play the sad music, the violins sounding like someone weeping. Some of the people from the crowd followed the coffin down the tunnel. Amy could see that most of them wore black armbands.

The rest of the people started to move away, heads bowed. Solemn, silent and sad.

'I wonder who died,' Rory whispered.

'Someone who had a lot of friends,' Amy whispered back.

'In a community like this, everyone knows everyone else,' the Doctor said. 'So that's not the most important question.'

'Then what is?' Amy asked.

There was as much sadness in the Doctor's eyes as he answered as in anyone else's there. 'Why did they die?'

CHAPTER 5
AFTER THE FUNERAL

The orchestra continued to play long after the funeral procession had gone. The Doctor, Amy and Rory sat on the edge of the stage and listened. The music was never really uplifting, but it became less solemn and sad.

Finally, after what seemed an age and when Amy was getting beyond fidgety and about to get up and leave, they drew to a close. Several of the children ran off into the fairground, carrying their trumpets and violins and other instruments with them.

The Doctor waved to a couple of boys as they ran past. 'That was terrific!' he called.

They stopped and thanked him.

'Ain't seen you round here before, Mister,' one of the boys said. He was about eleven years old with spiked up dark hair and a cheeky grin. 'You with the Galactic Fair?'

'No, just visiting. I'm the Doctor, and these are my friends, Amy and Rory.'

The boy was called Harby and his friend – fair-haired and slightly younger – was Vosh. Harby had a violin with him, in a dark case. Vosh played a trumpet that looked nearly as big as he was.

'So, where you from then?' Vosh asked.

'All over,' the Doctor told him. 'I'm the Everywhere Man. You play very well,' he went on. 'Whoever it was that's . . . passed away would have appreciated it.'

'The dead guy in the coffin you mean?' Harby said.

'I was kind of trying to avoid being so blunt.'

'It's all right.'

'So, who was he? Was he very old?' Amy asked.

'Rodge. Yeah, he was quite old.' Harby considered. 'About the same age as you,' he said, pointing at Rory.

'That is old,' the Doctor agreed. 'Old, old, old. If not even older. But not old enough for natural causes. Not old age natural causes. So how did he die?'

Harby shrugged.

'They wouldn't let us see,' Vosh told them. He was obviously disappointed. 'But,' he went on with gathering enthusiasm, 'my mate Benvo says he was all torn to pieces. Some sort of accident. Mum says that's why Off-Limits is off-limits.'

The Doctor nodded thoughtfully. 'Your mum sounds very wise.'

'You enjoying the funfair?' Rory asked brightly.

'It's OK,' Vosh said. 'The hook-a-ducklan is great. I've won a prize every time.'

Rory blinked and his smile became slightly

fixed. 'Really?'

'Be even better when the Death Ride opens,' Harby told them. 'Won't be long now. If they can get the health and safety stuff sorted.'

'Yes,' the Doctor agreed. 'Health and safety do tend to look a bit more closely at anything that has a title including the word "ride".'

Harby explained in excited tones, helped by a few interruptions from Vosh, that the Death Ride was a roller coaster that the Galactic Fair set up wherever they went. They built it into the landscape – or in this case into the tunnels. 'Must come in prefabricated sections that can be adapted to each location,' Rory said.

'They have all this track,' Vosh said. 'And, like, ramps and jumps and stuff.'

Harby nodded excitedly. 'They're using the steep tunnels, and even drilling through to other levels so they can do the bumps and drops. The best tunnels for that are all Off-Limits though.

But they're using tunnels close to Off-Limits when they can.'

'So why are some tunnels off-limits?' Amy wanted to know. 'What does that mean?'

'They're dangerous,' Harby explained. 'Not properly held up, or so old and worked out they might collapse. We're not allowed in them. No one is, except for inspection.'

They talked a bit longer, but the two boys were obviously getting keen to return to the fair. The sideshows had reopened and the stalls were doing brisk business. When the jugglers returned from their break and asked if the Doctor, Rory and Amy would please get off their stage, the boys said their goodbyes and hurried away.

'I can juggle,' the Doctor protested as he jumped down from the stage. 'Balls, skittles, plates, sonic screwdrivers. I can juggle anything.'

'Really?' one of the jugglers asked. He sounded genuinely interested – like he was about to ask the

Doctor to prove it.

'Really,' the Doctor insisted. 'But quite busy just now, actually. Maybe another time.'

After stopping several people to get directions, they were soon heading out of the fairground cavern and off down one of the tunnels.

'Hey, you know what?' Amy said. 'I think I'll stay here and look round a bit more. Maybe I can find out about the man who died. What sort of accident he had – if it was an accident.'

'You're not interested in the Death Ride?' the Doctor asked, disappointed.

'From what those kids said, it'll be like Rory setting up his train set. Only bigger.'

'What's wrong with that?' Rory asked. 'You often used to watch me setting up my train set.'

'Not through choice.' Amy said.

'I thought you enjoyed it.'

'I was bored almost to tears.'

Rory was aghast. 'You never said.'

'Well, I'm saying now. Train sets are for boys. Girls find them boring. I only stayed so you'd agree to come shopping in Gloucester.'

'Children!' the Doctor warned, grinning. 'Right then, Amy can stay here and investigate the poor dead Rodge. Rory and I are going to see how building the great big dangerous train set is going. Agreed?'

On their way to the tunnels where the Death Ride was being set up, the Doctor and Rory passed through part of the mining community. Rory was amazed at how the people lived. There were wooden buildings set up within the wider tunnels, fixed to the tunnel walls. It was like a Wild West frontier town, but underground.

More surprising and impressive was that some of the buildings were actually cut into the rock walls of the tunnels. The front of a house, complete with windows and door, turned out to be made of rock

— actually carved into the side of the tunnel. Behind it, the Doctor explained, a whole house would have been excavated, hacked out of the asteroid. That would have been a huge achievement in its own right — but the house was just the first of a whole tunnel-street of buildings.

'They've been here for a while,' the Doctor said. 'You humans get everywhere.'

'I wouldn't want to live here,' Rory decided. 'Never seeing sunlight, always underground. Everyone is so pale and there's dust everywhere. What if you were allergic to it? You'd be sneezing all the time.'

'Like everything, it depends what you're used to, what you know. These people don't know any other life. They probably think you're weird for wanting to look at an empty sky and spend time in bright light without a reassuring roof over your head, even when you're outdoors.'

'I suppose,' Rory said. But he wasn't convinced.

They could hear that they were approaching the work on the Death Ride. The clank of metal on metal and the rumble of the machinery echoed along the tunnel. They turned into yet another wide tunnel, and Rory could see a huge mesh of scaffolding rising up almost to the high roof.

Several men and women were manoeuvring metal rails into position on top of the scaffolding, which was shaped like an enormous 'S' lying on its side. The rails they had already positioned plunged down through a large, dark hole in the tunnel floor. The sound of more machinery came from the lower level.

Robot vehicles moved back and forth, bringing more scaffolding and rails. Everything was being supervised by a man wearing what looked like a circus ringmaster's uniform, complete with top hat.

'That'll be the Fat Controller,' Rory said.

'He doesn't look fat to me,' the Doctor said. 'I

think it's more likely to be the supervisor who sets up the Death Ride wherever the Galactic Fair goes.'

'Sort of what I meant, actually,' Rory told him.

A woman with her hair tied back in a ponytail and wearing the usual overalls of the local inhabitants came over to ask the Doctor and Rory what they were doing. She seemed happy enough to let them watch the work.

'Lots of the children wanted to watch when we started,' she told them. 'We had to make sure they didn't get in the way. But the novelty has worn off now. They'll be back as soon as the Death Ride opens.'

'And when will that be?' Rory asked.

'Very soon, I hope. This is the nearly the last section.'

'I was talking to someone earlier,' the Doctor said, 'who mentioned that the ride was supposed to go through some of the Off-Limits tunnels. Is that right?'

The woman pulled a face. 'That was the plan. It sort of fell through, though. But the Galactic Fair's Ride Master is still hoping we can get permission. That's him over there.' She pointed to the man in the ringmaster's outfit.

'And will you?' Rory asked.

'In my opinion? No chance. We've already got a replacement section planned that goes through the On-Limits section close by. It won't be as exciting, as it's not nearly so dark, and we can't get quite the same depth of plunge.'

'Shame,' Rory said, rather unconvincingly.

'So it'll soon be ready, then?' the Doctor said. 'Tickets available, trains leaving, kids screaming sort of thing?'

'Dicing with death on the highway to hell,' Rory added.

'We can't wait, can we, Rory?'

Rory was about to disagree, but the woman said, 'I'd better get back. We're bringing in the last few sections of track now. I want to get them in position before Perpetual Pete turns up and gives us more grief.'

'Perpetual Pete?' the Doctor asked.

'He's responsible for the safety of the mine. He's the one who won't let us go Off-Limits, even though Rodge said he was sure the tunnel we wanted to use was safe enough.'

'Rodge,' Rory remembered the name. 'Isn't he the man who died?'

'That's right. He was surveying the tunnel, although Pete told him he wasn't to go down there.'

'And that's where he died?'

'No. Like I said, that tunnel's safe. He was on his way back to file his report. Took a short cut through another Off-Limits. One that obviously wasn't safe. Perpetual Pete found the body.'

'Why's he called Perpetual Pete?' Rory asked, hoping he wasn't going to get another smart reply like he had from Clueless the Clown.

But the woman didn't seem interested in being funny. She wiped a grimy hand across her face and stifled a yawn. 'Because he's been here forever.'

'I think we should talk to this Perpetual Pete,' the Doctor said, watching the woman walk back to the scaffolding. 'As you and I both know, "forever" is a very long time.'

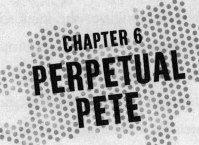

CHAPTER 6
PERPETUAL PETE

They spent a few minutes talking to some of the other people working on the Death Ride. The Doctor was interested to find out all he could about Perpetual Pete.

'If he's warning people away from the tunnels where poor Rodge died, maybe he knows more than he's saying.'

'Or,' Rory pointed out, 'it could be that he's warning people away from a dangerous tunnel where people have died because – get this – it's dangerous.'

The Doctor considered. 'Could be,' he admitted, but quickly went on: 'But we can't just guess without finding out the facts. Got to dot our Ts and cross our Is. No, Rory, not cross our eyes – stop that, really.'

An older man with a clipboard entered from a side tunnel. He looked annoyed, muttering and shaking his head as he checked his clipboard.

'Looks like a jobsworth,' Rory told the Doctor. 'I just bet that's Perpetual Pete.'

'Could be. Let's find out.'

The Doctor hurried over to the man. He stood on tiptoes to try to lean over and read what was on the clipboard. The man looked up slowly, frowning. The Doctor smiled and took a step backwards.

'Not good?' he asked.

The man shook his head again. 'Not good.'

Rory joined them.

'It's not good,' the Doctor told him solemnly.

'Not good,' Rory echoed. 'Right.'

'Perpetual Pete?' the Doctor asked.

'Absolutely,' the man agreed. 'Who else?' He jabbed his thumb over his shoulder, pointing back along the tunnel he'd just come down.

'Need a lift?' the Doctor asked. 'Or what?'

'What?' the man responded, puzzled.

'Perpetual Pete,' Rory started.

'Back there,' the man interrupted.

'What?' Rory said.

'Don't you start,' the Doctor muttered.

'Perpetual Pete,' the man said, 'is back there. He's insisting that the linkages be checked again. For about the thousandth time. And he's still not happy about the track going through that Off-Limits section of Green Nine. I've told him . . . ' the man said, nodding this time. 'Told him a hundred times.'

'A hundred?' the Doctor sounded impressed.

'At least.'

'We need to see Perpetual Pete. Down here, you say?'

The man didn't answer. He was making his way across to the scaffolding, still checking papers on his clipboard and shaking his head.

'Tell you what,' the Doctor said to Rory, 'you stay here and find out all you can about this Perpetual Pete. I'll go and talk to him.'

'Can't I come and talk to him too?' Rory asked.

The Doctor tilted his head to one side, looking at Rory with what might have been pity. 'And frighten the poor old man? You ask around here, and I'll go and talk to him. I bet he's lovely really. Just misunderstood.'

The Doctor strode off down the tunnel, hands in his pockets, as if he hadn't a care in the universe.

'I'm lovely really,' Rory said to the Doctor's back. 'Just misunderstood.'

The Doctor removed one hand from his pocket and waved. He didn't turn round. Rory watched him disappear into the distance, then sighed and looked for the man with the clipboard.

It was easy to spot Perpetual Pete. Apart from the fact that he looked like someone who was checking 'linkages' – whatever they were – he was also by far the oldest person the Doctor had seen since he arrived.

He was dressed much like the other citizens of Stanalan, in plain overalls with lots of useful pockets. The Doctor didn't like the dull grey colour much, but he envied the number of pockets. Pete was not a tall man. He looked stooped and slightly shrunken within his skin so that it no longer quite fit. His face was lined and sagging, and his straggly white beard had more hair in it than was left on the man's pale skull.

'Perpetual Pete, I assume.' The Doctor held out his hand.

'More complaints and interruptions, I assume.'

Perpetual Pete ignored the gesture.

He was intent on a device about the size and shape of a large TV remote control. It had a small screen set into the top half and buttons below. The Doctor peered over the old man's shoulder at the device. Pete turned slowly to see what the Doctor was doing, and the Doctor caught a whiff of sour breath. Actually, now he was close to the man, there was a definite niff coming from his whole body. The Doctor took a step back, wondering if there was such a thing as 'up-wind' in the tunnels.

'Checking the linkages, I see,' the Doctor said brightly.

Pete's already small, sunken eyes narrowed still further. 'What do you know about it?'

'Nothing at all. I mean, excuse me for asking, but what are these linkages you're checking?'

Pete gave a snort of mocking laughter. A string of spittle dribbled from the corner of his mouth and caught in his beard. 'You must be new here. Or stupid.'

'New – definitely new. And I was just asking. It's the only way to learn. I mean,' the Doctor went on, 'I assume that as there are no pit props, there must be some form of reinforcement to prevent the tunnels collapsing. There's no obvious forceshield, so it's probably a molecular bond that's woven into the top layer of rock when the tunnels are drilled out. The fluripsent light crystals are probably built into that same layer. So, is it molecular linkages you're checking on?'

Pete nodded. 'Top of the class, lad.' He turned away.

'So why do they need checking?' the Doctor wondered. 'Unless – ah! Do they become unstable over time? Molecular decay. But that would take . . . ' He counted rapidly on the fingers of both hands, several times. 'These tunnels must be very old,' he decided.

'Some of them. The older ones are off-limits until I've checked them.'

'Well, quite right. You wouldn't want people wandering about if the roof's going to fall in.'

Pete gave the Doctor a look that suggested this was more than obvious.

'Wouldn't want a Death Ride rollercoaster going through them either, I'd guess.'

'Is that why you're here?' Pete demanded suspiciously. 'You one of the fair people, come to ask about Green Nine again? Because the answer's still no.'

The Doctor held up his hands in mock surrender. 'Not me, no siree. I'm not any sort of people. But if this Green Nine section is unstable, can't you just realign the molecules and re-bond the membrane? I assume that's what you do when the linkages break down.'

'You know all about it then, do you?'

The Doctor just smiled.

'Well, Mr Clever . . . '

'It's Doctor, not Mr,' the Doctor told him. He smiled again. 'Doctor Clever.'

'Well, whoever you are, if it was just a case of the linkages, then yes, we could go to the expense and trouble and hassle of re-bonding the tunnel. It would take longer than they can wait, but we could. But unless we're now going to check the Off-Limits for oxygen seepage, pressure leaks, toxic gas incursion, structural instability and a hundred other things that can go wrong with a tunnel, there'd be no point really. Would there?'

The Doctor nodded. 'Suppose not. Fair point, actually. Good point even. So, these Off-Limits places, they're tunnels that aren't needed any more, and so they just get minimum maintenance and you check they're not going to destabilise the rest of the asteroid, but otherwise don't bother to keep them too safe? Hence "Off-

Limits" because no one's allowed down there except, I assume, for you. To do your checking.'

'Absolutely right. So how about you let me get on with it?'

'Sure thing. Absolutely. Only . . . '

Perpetual Pete sighed. 'What?' he asked with forced patience.

'Only, how come poor dead Rodge was found in an Off-Limits tunnel if no one's allowed down there?'

'Rules don't stop people being stupid.'

'And if the tunnel was unstable and he died in a rockfall, or from lack of oxygen, or toxic gas… How come his body was ripped to pieces?'

'Is that what they're saying?'

'You found his body,' the Doctor said quietly. 'What are you saying?'

'My job's to keep the main tunnels safe, and warn people which sections are Off-Limits. I'm saying he shouldn't have been down there.

I'm saying it doesn't matter how he died, it just goes to show that off-limits means off-limits. I'm saying that sending a fairground ride close to areas that are Off-Limits is dangerous and irresponsible and if someone pays me to do a job they should listen to my advice.'

The Doctor nodded. 'Doesn't answer my question, but all very reasonable. Who does pay you to do the job by the way? Just out of interest.'

'He's paid by the company,' the man with the clipboard said. His name, he'd told Rory, was Korl. 'Perpetual Pete is the Health and Safety Executive. Every mine has to have one. Usually they only stay for a few months before they transfer out. It's a boring and unrewarding job that new recruits do before being promoted to management roles.'

'But not Perpetual Pete?'

'He's been here longer than I have. Hence his nickname.'

'And how long have you been here?'

Korl laughed. 'I was born here.' His laughter died away. 'Funny,' he said. 'I never thought about it, but I'm one of the most senior miners now, and Pete's been old for as long as I can remember. Maybe we should call him "Ancient Pete."'

Rory didn't think he'd find out much more, and Korl had work to do. Perpetual Pete evidently kept himself very much to himself. Aside from the mystery of just how long he'd been here and how old he was, he wasn't a very popular person. The miners generally felt he was too strict in his safety rulings and tended to keep tunnels Off-Limits when there was no real need – tunnels that could make things easier for the miners if they were opened again. And he was smelly.

The quickest way back to the fair, Korl had told Rory, was to follow the Death Ride tracks for about twenty minutes until he reached the "main concourse". Apparently he couldn't miss this, as it was the widest tunnel in the asteroid. In Rory's experience, 'You can't miss it,' usually meant the opposite.

But he never got that far. Death was waiting for Rory along the way.

CHAPTER 7
DEATH IN THE TUNNELS

The fair was soon as lively and noisy as it had been before the funeral procession. Amy was hoping to see Garvo and Drexxon again. She still wasn't convinced the monkey-like creature was as happy and contented as Garvo said. She'd have liked to watch them again to reassure herself, but they were not outside their tent and no one had seen them since the procession.

People were happy to talk to Amy – people working at the fair, and people there to enjoy themselves. But none of them knew much about the death. Rodge had been a popular and well-known character. Everyone knew he had ventured into Off-Limits. He was the sort of person who was always looking for short cuts in the way he worked, so actually taking a short cut was completely in character for him. The general feeling was that he had been killed in a freak rockfall.

'That happens in Off-Limits,' a woman told Amy. 'That's why they're Off-Limits, of course. We all do it, we all take the odd short cut. But, well, some tunnels are more Off-Limits than others. Rodge knew he was taking a risk, poor soul.'

'He was always a bit reckless,' an older man confided. 'Wouldn't wish it on anyone, but if you take that sort of risk . . . ' He shook his head and whistled through his teeth. 'Only have to get it wrong once, you know. Don't you go Off-Limits, now. Don't you even think about it.'

Amy thanked him for his advice. 'Are there many deaths in Off-Limits areas, many accidents?'

The man considered. 'Not many. It's years

since Jemmie nearly suffocated when an Off-Limits sealed itself off after an oxygen leak while he was playing hide and seek . . . No, some say Perpetual Pete is too strict about Off-Limits. But this just goes to show what can happen if you're not strict enough. Without Perpetual Pete there'd be a lot more accidents, you mark my words, young woman.'

'But it's not that unusual?'

The man nodded sadly. 'Tragic, but accidents do happen. A death though? That's extremely unlikely to happen again. Especially now, people will be even more wary of the Off-Limits. There won't be any more accidental deaths for years, you can take it from me.'

Another dead body?' the Doctor asked. 'You sure? No, sorry, forget that. You work in a hospital. Of course you're sure.'

Rory was doubled over, out of breath. He'd

run all the way, hoping to find the Doctor still with Perpetual Pete – which he had. He'd paused only to shout to Korl that he'd found a body.

Perpetual Pete was anxious to know exactly where Rory had discovered the corpse. Rory tried to hold his breath while the smelly old man was talking, but it was difficult. As he led them back through the tunnels to where the body was, he described how he'd followed the Death Ride tracks through several tunnels. Sometimes they rose steeply up into a higher level before plunging down again. But it was easy enough to follow the route.

'It was just luck,' Rory explained. 'I stopped to get my bearings. Just by where the track disappears underground. It goes down this deep, dark hole, really steep.' He shuddered at the thought of experiencing the ride. The Doctor's obvious eagerness didn't improve his feeling. 'Anyway, there's a tunnel running off the other way at that point. I thought, if the ride turns while it's down a level, maybe it'll come up again in that tunnel. There's a flashing red sign that says "Off-Limits" at the entrance to the tunnel, but I thought I'd check anyway. Just in case.' He swallowed, catching sight of Pete's angry glare. 'So I went to look – just a few steps. That's all.'

'Green Eight,' Perpetual Pete said. 'They wanted to give it a hairpin turn there and go all the way through to Green Nine. No way,' he added, shaking his head emphatically. 'The signs are there for a reason. You shouldn't have gone down there. It's not safe at all.'

'Obviously not,' the Doctor agreed.

'She was lying close to the tunnel wall. There isn't a lot of light at that point – those crystal things don't seem to work in that tunnel. But there was enough to catch her face. Her eyes . . .' Rory shuddered again. He'd seen a lot of death, but he would never get used to it.

'We don't recharge the crystals in the Off-Limits tunnels. Was it another rockfall?' Pete asked. But there was something in the way he asked it that made Rory suspect he already knew the answer.

'Possibly,' Rory said cautiously. He glanced at the Doctor before going on. 'But it looked more to me like she'd been scratched and bitten.'

'Do you have rats in the tunnels?' the Doctor asked.

Perpetual Pete shook his head. 'No,' he said. 'Not rats.'

'I'm guessing you don't usually have this sort of trouble,' the Doctor said.

'Not usually. But I'll tell you something,' Pete said, spraying Rory with a fine mist of spittle, 'if they go ahead with that Death Ride, we're likely to have a whole lot more unpleasantness than you can imagine.'

'Oh, I can actually imagine quite a lot of

unpleasantness,' the Doctor said. 'Still, you could be right. You could very well be right.'

Amy heard the sad sound of the harmonica before she saw them. Garvo and Drexxon were once more performing outside their tent, and a small crowd had already gathered.

'They're good, aren't they?'

Amy turned to find that Harby and Vosh, the boys from the orchestra, were standing close by.

'They're brilliant,' she told them.

'Weird, but good,' Harby agreed. 'We've been waiting for them to come back for ages.'

'Come back from where?'

'Who knows?' Vosh said. 'They just go off. Maybe they just go for something to eat or drink.'

'Or maybe the rumours are true,' Harby said.

'What rumours are those?' Amy wondered.

The boys moved closer, checking that no one

else was listening.

'Walking the tunnels at night,' Harby whispered.

'People have heard them,' Vosh added. 'My mate Lymm says she heard Garvo's harmonica echoing down an Off-Limits the other night shift. Real spooky, she said it was.'

'I can imagine. But so what if Garvo plays his music at night and goes for a walk?'

'It's just weird,' Harby said dismissively. 'Probably part of the act. Like, getting attention and pretending to be mysterious and stuff.'

'Probably,' Amy agreed.

Together with her two young friends, Amy wriggled her way to the front of the gathering crowd. Drexxon was capering up and down on his leash as the haunting music filled the air. Amy tried to catch the creature's eye. Did it remember her? Could she tell from its furry little expression whether it was really happy? She wondered whether Drexxon actually danced instinctively to the music, or whether he had been trained – she hated to think how that might be done. More stick than carrot, she suspected.

Maybe it was the tone of the music, but Amy suddenly felt an overwhelming sense of sadness for the creature. What choice could it possibly have while it was attached – shackled – to its master? It occurred to her that there was one way she could find out for sure if Drexxon was happy, or if he would rather run away and escape from Garvo. Without even thinking about it, she found she had edged closer to where Drexxon was now jumping up and down like an excited pogo stick.

She would have to be quick. If Garvo guessed what she was up to, he'd stop playing and take Drexxon away before Amy could do anything. But she was almost within reach now. The creature tilted its head to one side slightly as it looked at Amy. It seemed like it recognised her, which would help.

The music was coming to an end. The crowd was getting ready to applaud. People were nodding to each other and murmuring praise. Amy forced herself to smile. She held her hands out to Drexxon as if to compliment him, and as she had hoped, the little creature reached back to her.

As quickly, but gently, as she could, Amy caught Drexxon's paw. It was warm and soft, but she could feel the hardness of the claws even while they were retracted. She only needed a moment. It was easier than she thought. She expected the leash to be firmly attached. But it was only loosely slipped over Drexxon's wrist.

Amy pulled the leash carefully away from Drexxon's wrist and tossed it away.

'It's all right,' she said. 'You're safe now.'

But her words were drowned out by the screams.

'What have you done?' Harby shouted.

'He's gone mad,' Vosh added.

They didn't mean Drexxon. The creature was regarding Amy curiously. It made no effort to escape. If anything, it looked angry.

But the effect on Garvo was very different. He collapsed to his knees, hands clasped to his head as if in pain. His harmonica fell to the ground as he screamed and shrieked. His whole body was shaking. His face was contorted with pain. As Amy watched, he fell sideways, curling into a ball as he continued to cry out.

CHAPTER 8
BROKEN LINKS

Drexxon immediately scampered back towards Garvo. The creature looked down at the writhing man, and Amy could see what looked almost like pity in its eyes. Its furry little paws tugged at the thin leash that was still attached to Garvo's wrist. It pulled on the leash, reeling it in as quickly as it could. As soon as it caught hold of the loop at the end, it slipped it back over its wrist.

Amy was amazed. But she was also pleased. Despite her fears and worries, the creature really did seem to value its relationship with its human master. Though perhaps, Amy thought, it was more of a partnership, as Garvo had told her.

After all, she now knew from her own experience, Drexxon could have removed the leash from its wrist at any time.

She turned her attention to Garvo. Having got over their shock at his collapse, several people from the crowd had hurried to help. Amy suddenly felt incredibly guilty about the distress she'd caused the man. She was sure he had reacted to her 'releasing' Drexxon. Had he really worried he might lose the creature – his friend? Or was it painful to break the link between them? Just as Garvo reacted to the way the leash conveyed Garvo's music, did Garvo feel something from Drexxon that it was unpleasant for him to lose?

'What was all that about?' Harby asked. 'Is he OK?'

Garvo seemed to be recovering. He waved away the people trying to help and got back to his feet.

'I'm so sorry.' His voice sounded strained and tired. 'I had a bit of a shock. The connection between myself and Drexxon – it's what drives the music, the dance. What keeps us working so well together as an act.'

Aware that the people near her were beginning to look at Amy rather suspiciously, she backed away. How many of them had seen her slip Drexxon's leash off the creature's wrist? How many of those people had realised that it must have been the cause of Garvo's dramatic collapse? He'd just told them, after all, that breaking the connection had caused him pain and upset.

'See you,' she said quietly to Harby and Vosh, and backed away through the crowd.

The harmonica music started up again and people turned back to see the show. As she turned and slipped away, the last Amy saw of the show was Drexxon – its deep-set, dark eyes fixed on her accusingly.

The body that Rory had found was a female mining engineer who'd been part of the team helping to set up the Death Ride. The best theory seemed to be that she had wandered into the Off-Limits tunnel, and been caught in a rockfall.

'An extremely rare rockfall,' the Doctor pointed out. 'An extremely rare rockfall that didn't show up on your seismic registers.'

'They aren't tuned to be as sensitive in Off-Limits areas,' Perpetual Pete pointed out.

The Doctor, Rory and Pete watched as the body was stretchered away by medics. The 'Off-Limits' sign at the mouth of the tunnel flashed on and off, striping the stretcher with red light.

'So,' the Doctor went on, 'an extremely rare and small rockfall that left her with no crush injuries, just those scratches.'

'And then,' Rory added, 'she staggered back here, and died of heart failure.'

'Delayed shock,' Perpetual Pete grumbled.

'Very delayed,' the Doctor said. He peered down the dimly lit Off-Limits tunnel. 'Can't see any sign of a rockfall from here. Let's go and find it.'

Perpetual Pete grabbed the Doctor's collar and hauled him back with surprising strength. 'No one goes down there,' he spat. Literally.

'Why not?' the Doctor demanded. 'You didn't even want the medics to go and retrieve the body, and it was only a few metres down the tunnel.'

'It's Off-Limits. That's why.'

'There's got to be more to it than that.' Rory told him.

'Don't you get it?' Pete said. 'It's dangerous. That's why the tunnels are Off-Limits. It's a safety measure, and people need to understand that Off-Limits means Off-Limits.'

'Well,' the Doctor announced, 'that tunnel looks safe enough to me. The roof's secure, the walls are sound. There's no sign of damage or stress. What is it that makes you so certain that going down that tunnel is dangerous?'

Perpetual Pete's face had reddened with anger. For a moment he was so furious he could scarcely speak. When he did, his voice was a low rumble, 'What about a dead body? Doesn't that suggest at least an element of risk to you? Or are you going to tell her husband and kids that the place she died is completely safe and there's nothing at all to worry about and you're happy she was down there?'

Rory swallowed. 'Fair point, I think actually, Doctor.'

The Doctor was silent for a moment. Then he nodded slowly. 'Well, it was good to meet you, Mr Pete. I don't know what you're hiding, but I don't like it.'

'I'm hiding nothing,' Pete said. But he suddenly looked very uncomfortable.

'And if anyone else dies – anyone at all,' the

Doctor went on, 'I shall blame you. Come on Rory – it's candyfloss time.'

'You think he did it?' Rory asked as they hurried back towards the fair.

'He was with me, he can't have killed that woman.'

'But he knows more than he's saying.'

'Has to. Because he's not saying anything.'

'He's a nasty, rude, smelly, old man,' Rory said. 'He's got to be behind whatever's going on.'

The Doctor glanced sideways at him. 'Way to go, Sherlock. Never mind the lack of evidence, the man stinks. So he has to be the villain.'

'So what do you think?' Rory demanded.

'I think we should find Amy. I think I need more candyfloss. I think everything about this stinks, not just Perpetual Pete. And for what it's worth, evidence or not, I think you're right. He's a nasty, rude, smelly, old man and he's got to be the villain.'

Amy didn't really feel comfortable at the fair. It seemed like everyone was looking at her. She could imagine them whispering to each other: 'Look, there goes that mad woman who caused all the trouble with Garvo and Drexxon.'

She tried to ignore it, but the feeling just kept growing. There was only one thing for it, she decided – she'd have to go and apologise to Garvo. She ought to. It was the right thing to do. She'd been wrong and she'd caused him pain and grief, and however embarrassing it might be she should go and get it over with.

It didn't surprise her that Garvo and Drexxon were taking a break from performing. What did surprise her was what she saw as she looked round to try to work out the quickest way out of the cavern and the best way to try to find the Doctor and Rory.

At first it was just a blurred movement, glimpsed out of the corner of her eye. But when she turned, her eye drawn to the movement, Amy was just in time to see the distinctive furry shape of Drexxon disappearing furtively into the nearest tunnel. The only reason she'd been in time to see the creature was that Drexxon had paused to look round, as if checking it wasn't being watched, before slipping round the corner and out of sight.

Assuming that Garvo must be with Drexxon, Amy hurried after the creature. But when she got to the tunnel, she could see no sign of anyone. She ran down the tunnel, hoping to catch up. At one point, she thought she saw a shadow scuttling ahead of her. But it certainly wasn't Garvo.

After a while she gave up and slowed to a halt. As she caught her breath, Amy saw that another, smaller tunnel led off to one side. A sign saying "Off-Limits" flickered as if the bulb was about to go. Was it her imagination, or could she see something moving down there?

She stared into the near darkness of the side tunnel for a while, but she could make out nothing. Her best bet was to get back to the fair, she decided. Rory and the Doctor would look for her there – they might already be looking for her. And if and when Garvo returned from another harmonica-playing tour of the tunnels, or whatever he was up to, she could apologise to him properly.

The Doctor and Rory were eating candyfloss when Amy found them.

'Having fun?' she asked.

'Not really,' Rory told her.

'He found a dead body,' the Doctor explained. 'That's never much fun.'

Between them, the Doctor and Rory described what had happened, then Amy filled them in on the little she had learned.

'So, we're off to explore Off-Limits tunnels

then?' she asked.

'Seems the best bet,' Rory admitted. He didn't sound excited by the idea.

'Great,' Amy said. 'Oh, hang on . . . ' A thought occurred to her. 'I just want to check if Garvo's back. He wasn't there just now, but I want to talk to him.'

'What about?' Rory asked.

'Oh, you know – stuff.'

'Stuff?'

'Yeah. Stuff. Won't be long.'

How long Amy stood in the doorway of the tent staring at the scene inside, she had no idea. But it was long enough for the Doctor and Rory to come and find her to see what was happening.

Amy said nothing. She just stood aside so they could see.

The tent was almost empty, like a small bedsit – with just a table and chair and a mattress on the ground for a bed. Lying on the mattress was Garvo. One hand trailed off the side of the mattress. His harmonica lay where it had fallen from his grasp. The thin leash, one end still attached to his wrist, lay coiled nearby. The loop that usually enclosed Drexxon's wrist was empty and lying curled like a question mark on the ground. Garvo's eyes were wide open, staring unseeing at the roof of the tent.

CHAPTER 9
MASTER AND SLAVE

Rory ran to the mattress and checked Garvo's pulse.

Amy stood watching, her knuckles pressed to her teeth. 'I let Drexxon off the leash,' she confessed. 'Just for a moment, for a few seconds, that's all. Did I do this? Is he . . . ?'

'He's got a pulse,' Rory said. He could feel the faintest throbbing under his finger as he held Garvo's wrist. 'He's alive. He's breathing, look.'

The Doctor leaned over Garvo, staring into the man's eyes. He waved. No response. So he pulled the most outrageous face and blew a raspberry. There was still no response.

'What's wrong with him?' Amy asked.

'No sense of humour by the look of it,' the Doctor said.

'Coma of some sort?' Rory suggested. 'Slow pulse, shallow breathing, no awareness . . . '

'Loss of free will,' the Doctor said. 'How does that happen? Or is it something he chose to do to himself? Like taking medicine. A healing process maybe?'

'Oh, come on,' Rory said, 'you can't ask us to believe that someone could put themselves into a coma at will so their body can recover from some trauma.' He caught the Doctor's smug expression. 'Right, self-induced coma – definitely a possibility.'

Amy was nervously twisting the leash between her fingers. She didn't even seem to realise she'd picked it up.

'Let me see that,' the Doctor said, jumping over the mattress and just clearing Garvo's unmoving body. He sat down on the ground and examined the leash. A moment later, he had his sonic screwdriver out and was hard at work.

'It's just a bit of plastic, probably with a metal core,' Rory pointed out.

'Oh, it's much more than that.' The Doctor didn't look up. 'You say you slipped it off Drexxon's wrist?' he asked Amy, still examining the leash. 'And Garvo didn't like that?'

'He went ape,' Amy confirmed. 'OK, maybe not the best expression given he's got an alien space monkey as a pet, but he lost it big time.'

'Angry?' Rory asked.

'Maybe . . . ' the Doctor conceded. 'If he thought you'd released Drexxon.'

'But Drexxon went straight back to him,' Amy pointed out.

'There'd be confusion, maybe panic, when this link was broken.' The Doctor held up the leash for them to see. 'Perhaps Drexxon's instinct was to seek out comfort in the only way it knew, with the only person it recognised.'

'What are you saying?' Rory asked. 'That's just a leash, isn't it? Or is it?'

The Doctor tossed it away and leaped to his feet. 'Far more than that. It's a neuronic control system. Nasty thing.'

Amy frowned. 'So, what does it do?'

'Put simply, for us simple people, it links two individuals – or a person and an alien space monkey – so that one can control the other by sending mental signals down the cable inside. Hypnotism by wire.'

Amy gave a snort that combined both satisfaction and outrage. 'I knew he had some hold over the poor thing.' She kicked at the mattress, where Garvo did not react.

'Careful, Amy,' Rory warned.

'I told you the poor thing was a slave.'

'You did,' the Doctor admitted. 'We should

trust your instincts.'

'He must have run off while Garvo's getting his kip.' Amy sighed. 'The poor little thing can't have had to survive on its own for years. It must be so scared and alone.'

She pushed aside the flap of material that formed the door to the tent.

'Where are you going?' Rory asked.

'To find Drexxon. I saw him earlier, heading off down one of the tunnels. I thought Garvo must be with him, but obviously not. You coming?'

She didn't wait for an answer, but stepped out of the tent, allowing the flap to fall back into place.

The Doctor was staring at his sonic screwdriver, brow furrowed in thought. 'Rory . . .'

'Going after Amy,' Rory called from the mouth of the tent.

'Good. Bring her back here – quickly!'

Rory caught the urgency in his voice. 'Problem?'

'Just get her.'

There was no sign of Amy. By the time Rory left the tent, she had already disappeared into the crowds. Rather than go rushing off in a random direction he stood on tiptoe and tried to spot Amy's distinctive hair. Clueless the Clown waved to him and Rory forced a smile as he waved back.

'Where is she?' the Doctor demanded from right behind Rory's ear, making him jump.

'Can't see her. She'll be halfway to wherever by now. You know what she's like.'

'I know what she's like,' the Doctor agreed. 'But she doesn't know what Drexxon's like.'

'The poor little monkey-boy that Garvo kept enslaved. She'll smother him with sympathy when she finds him.'

'Ugh,' the Doctor winced. 'I hope not.

Because things are not always what they seem. And in this case they most certainly are not what they seem.'

Something in the Doctor's tone made Rory feel suddenly anxious and cold. 'What do you mean?'

'Checked the readings. The control flow is reversed.'

'And in English?'

'Rory, Rory, Rory,' the Doctor said. 'We thought the control leash was being used by Garvo to make Drexxon do what he wanted, right?'

'Right.' Rory saw the Doctor's expression. 'Wrong?' he guessed again.

'Wrong. Big time wrong.'

'Then what?' But even as he asked the question, Rory realised the answer. 'You mean, Drexxon is making Garvo do what he wants? Alien space monkey enslaves the will of poor human musician?'

The Doctor nodded. 'Alien space monkey

puts poor human musician into a coma so it can wander off for a bit and do what it likes without losing control when the leash comes off.'

'Can we wake him up?'

'Not safely. It takes time to wake someone from that state and then we'd have to wean him off the control. That could be tricky too, especially if he's been under it for a while. Amy told us what happened when she broke the control link – Garvo had a breakdown. The confusion and anger and pain in his mind as he struggled to cope with what's been done to him must have been . . . extreme.'

'No wonder Drexxon put the leash back on quick time.'

'So now we have a nasty vicious space monkey creature with sharp claws running loose in the tunnels,' the Doctor said.

They both thought about it for a moment.

'We have to find Amy – now!' they both said.

'She mentioned seeing Drexxon go down a tunnel,' Rory reminded the Doctor.

'But which one? There are dozens. If someone saw her, we'd be able to follow.'

'Who do we ask?' Rory wondered.

'Everyone!'

They ran through the fair, calling Amy's name and asking anyone and everyone if they had seen her. Before long, several people were helping with the search. Clueless the Clown strode above everyone, hoping to spot Amy's distinctive hair.

'Flame red hair?' asked a fire-eater. 'I'll certainly help look. Us flamers have to stick together.'

The man's own head was completely bald. Rory wondered for a moment if he'd burned his hair off learning his trade. Best not to think about it, he decided. He certainly wasn't going to ask.

Harby and Vosh came running up to them to know what was happening.

'Your friend Amy?' Harby asked.

'Not just my friend . . . ' Rory started, but the Doctor nudged him to be quiet and let Harby finish.

'She headed off towards Yellow Nineteen.'

'About ten minutes ago,' Vosh added.

'You want us to show you?' Harby asked. He sounded reluctant. 'Only they're saying the Death Ride's nearly finished and we wanted to take a look at the starting gate.'

'I know Yellow Nineteen,' the fire-eater said. 'It's this way.'

'Thanks for your help,' the Doctor told the two boys.

'Is there a reward if you find her?' Vosh asked.

'Absolutely,' the Doctor assured him. 'I'll get Amy to give you a kiss.'

Vosh stared at him as if he was mad.

'Oh yuck!'

Amy's instincts told her that the poor Drexxon would keep to the shadows and the darker tunnels. That was why she hadn't managed to spot him when she followed him before. He must be so frightened.

The Off-Limits tunnels she'd reached before seemed like a good place to start. OK, it was Off-Limits, but Drexxon wouldn't know that. Provided she went slowly and carefully, what danger could there really be?

'Are you there?' she called, as she made her cautious way along the tunnel. 'Drexxon – can you hear me? It's all right, I won't hurt you. I know what's been going on, what's really been going on. I just want to help you, OK?'

There was a scuffling from further down the tunnel. As she approached, Amy could see a section of scaffolding sticking out from the side wall. The Death Ride extended into the tunnel before curving sharply away again – round and down through the floor. This was probably one of the sections that Perpetual Pete had got so worked up about.

The scuffling sound came again. Amy was sure she could see a pair of eyes glinting in the shadows beneath the scaffolding.

'There you are.' She stooped down and reached out into the darkness. 'I know you're there. It's all right. Everything's going to be fine.'

Drexxon edged out of the shadows and into the dim light. The creature seemed more confident than Amy had expected. It regarded her through its small, dark eyes. It raised a paw. With a staccato 'click', claws sprang out from the end of the paw.

Amy backed away, straightening up. This wasn't right. She took a step backwards – but too late.

With a snarl of rage, the creature hurled itself at her. Sharp teeth glinted as they caught the light. Its savage claws slashed down at Amy.

CHAPTER 10
THE SECRET OF THE ASTEROID

Amy fell backwards. Claws slashed down close to her face, but somehow she managed to avoid them. She thrust her hands out, grabbing the Drexxon by the throat. The creature's fur was like steel wool, cutting into her hands as she struggled to hold it away and keep clear of the savage claws.

But it was a struggle she couldn't win. The Drexxon was incredibly strong – far stronger than it looked. With every second the claws came closer. She could smell the creature's warm, unpleasant breath. She could hear its squeals of triumph.

Then suddenly it was gone. Amy rolled away, catching sight of the Drexxon hurtling through the air like a football. It struck the rock wall behind the scaffolding and slid to the ground.

Above Amy, Rory was hopping on his left leg, trying to massage his right foot.

'That hurt!' he complained. 'I'm not kicking one of those again!'

Amy would have laughed with relief. But the Drexxon was recovering. It seemed to gather itself, ready to attack again. Amy crawled backwards, yelling at Rory to watch out. Other people were running up now – the Doctor, several of the people from the fair and a couple of miners in overalls.

The Drexxon emerged from beneath the scaffolding. It stared at the people grouped round it with obvious anger, hissing through its sharp little teeth.

'Don't go near it,' the Doctor warned. 'It's cornered and dangerous. It's certainly not a pussycat, so don't even think about trying to stroke it.'

'As if,' Amy muttered.

With an echoing roar of rage, that seemed as if it must have come from a much larger animal, the Drexxon attacked again. It hurtled towards the assembled people. Most of them scattered – knocking the hopping Rory over. Only the Doctor stood his ground. The Doctor and one other man – a man stripped to the waist, holding a firebrand. Amy expected him to try to ward off the attacking creature with the burning torch he was holding. Instead, to her astonishment, he raised the firebrand above his head, turned it so the burning end was downwards and then stuck the firebrand in his mouth.

'Don't try this at home,' the Doctor warned,

stepping out of the way.

The Drexxon leaped at the firer-eater.

The fire-eater pulled the torch from his mouth, and blew a stream of flame at the Drexxon. It gave a shriek of pain and anger, dropping to the rock floor. The fire-eater stepped forward, ready to spew fire at it again. But the creature scampered away into the shadows. Amy could hear the click of its claws on the ground as it disappeared.

Assured by the Doctor that there was nothing more to see, the people slowly drifted away. Some of them were frightened by what they'd seen, others assumed it was all part of a show staged by the people from the fair. There was even some applause. The Doctor thanked the fire-eater profusely. Amy ran to find Rory – who was still hopping about and complaining about his foot.

'I mean, the thing looks like a furry football.

A furry football with teeth and claws, but even so. It certainly doesn't feel like one.'

Amy hugged him. 'Never mind. Thanks anyway. I love you even if you can't walk. Or play football. Should have left it to the Doctor.'

Rory managed to stand up long enough to give her a hug back.

'So, what's going on?' Amy demanded. 'And what's the plan now?'

'Drexxon was controlling Garvo – he was the slave, not the poor ickle cute monkey space alien,' Rory explained.

'And as for a plan,' the Doctor added, 'I need to talk to the one person who might know what's really going on. And here he comes now.'

Amy turned to see where the Doctor was looking. A figure was approaching along the tunnel, shuffling into the dim light.

'You know this tunnel is Off-Limits,' the old man wheezed.

'Absolutely,' the Doctor told him. 'Amy — meet Perpetual Pete. He's going to tell us all he knows about the Drexxons, and why this perfectly safe tunnel that's not in any danger of collapse — along with so many others — is Off-Limits.'

'Drexxons?' Perpetual Pete asked. Even in the dim light, he seemed to have gone as pale as his straggly white beard. 'I don't know what you're talking about.'

'Yeah, you do,' the Doctor told him. 'It's time you told us why you're so desperate to keep people away from certain parts of this asteroid and out of specific tunnels. It's time for you to tell us what you're doing here. And who you really are.'

'I've been here, on this asteroid, for a very long time,' Perpetual Pete said.

'So I gathered,' Rory said.

The Doctor glared at him to be quiet. The four of them — the Doctor, Amy, Rory and

Perpetual Pete were sitting on the tunnel floor close to the scaffolding as Pete told his story. Everyone else had returned to the fair or gone back to work.

'I've been here longer than anyone else knows or can remember,' Pete went on, as if Rory had not spoken. 'They think my job is to keep them safe. And they're right.' He broke off into thoughtful silence.

'But you're not keeping them safe in the way they think,' the Doctor prompted.

'No, I'm not,' Perpetual Pete confessed. 'I don't work for the Interplanetary Mining Corporation who own this asteroid and pay their wages. The executives at IMC don't care about the safety of their workers. In fact, they'd rather the miners did work in unsafe tunnels if it makes them more money.'

'So who does pay you?' Amy asked.

'I was given a job, and the means to carry it

out, before there even was a mine here. Before IMC and the other corporations even existed. I tried to warn off the first pioneers and prospectors. When they discovered trisilicate and the company's drilling robots moved in, I did my best to steer them away from a particular part of this asteroid. And I succeeded. But then, when they'd worked out one area they moved on to another and then another. It's been a constant battle to steer them away from certain tunnels – tunnels that were here already, like this one. Tunnels drilled for a very different purpose over seven hundred years ago, when I was a young man.'

'But why?' Amy asked. 'Why did you want to keep people away from these tunnels?' She glanced round nervously.

'Because of the Drexxons,' the Doctor said. 'Am I right, or am I totally and absolutely correct?'

Perpetual Pete was nodding. 'Almost a

thousand years ago, the Drexxons rampaged through this whole sector of space. That was long before the humans came.' He smiled, chipped and yellowed teeth glinting. 'Does it surprise you to learn I'm not human?'

'There's a lot of it about, actually,' Rory said.

'Oh.' Pete seemed disappointed not to have provoked gasps of astonishment. 'Well, never mind. Anyway, as I say, the Drexxons rampaged through space. They attacked planet after planet, killing and destroying. Not for any reason – they didn't want an empire or wealth or power. They just did it because they could. Because they enjoyed it. And you know, that made it worse.'

'I bet,' the Doctor murmured.

'Finally we managed to round them up. A combined force, led by General Petrovnal, defeated the Drexxons. We offered them a planetary system of their own if they'd just stay there and live in peace. But even against such huge odds, they wouldn't surrender. After a terrible battle, a battle that lasted for over a decade, we managed to trap them all inside a Perpetuity Chamber.'

'And what's one of those?' Amy asked.

'A prison,' the Doctor said. 'A cage. Inside, time stops. Everything is held in stasis – unchanging. In perpetuity – forever. But open the lid . . . '

'We hid the Chamber so it would never be found and the Drexxons would never again emerge to threaten our lands and our children,' Pete told them.

'Guessing you hid it on a bleak, barren asteroid that no one in their right mind would ever be interested in,' the Doctor said.

Pete nodded. 'It seemed like a good idea at the time. The Chamber is very fragile. Once positioned and sealed within a protective vault, it cannot be moved, or the barriers break down and the Chamber opens. There was a chance, just a chance, that someone might one day stumble across it. So I was appointed its guardian. My job – my life – is to make sure the Chamber is never opened.'

'And I thought you were just a rude, smelly, old man,' Rory said. 'Oh – sorry.'

Pete glared at him. 'You'd smell too if you were several hundred years old.'

'Um, not necessarily,' the Doctor said quickly, gesturing for Rory to make no further comment of his own. 'At least, I hope not. Can we move on?'

'So now a Drexxon has found this Perpetuity Chamber,' Amy said.

'One must have escaped,' Pete agreed. 'It waited all these years. They are incredibly long-lived. I imagine it has been searching for the Chamber, using the Galactic Fair as cover for its search across the cosmos. They may be savage and vicious, but they are also very patient.'

'Poor Garvo probably isn't the first human the Drexxon has hooked up with,' the Doctor guessed.

'But that Drexxon,' Amy said, 'it's just a space monkey. I mean, it's nasty and dangerous but surely it's not big enough to cause much trouble.'

'From what you tell me, that is a small one,' Pete said. 'A child. That must be how we missed it.'

'So, how big do they grow, exactly?' Rory asked.

'An adult Drexxon would fit in this tunnel,' Pete said. He glanced up at the roof – five metres above their heads. 'Just.'

'But what's the thing doing?' Rory wondered. 'Why's it killing people?'

'Because that's what it does, what it enjoys,'

Pete snapped. 'Weren't you listening?'

'There must be more to it than that,' the Doctor said. 'Maybe Rodge and the other victim found it sneaking about down in the tunnels. But what can it have been doing that it didn't want them to reveal?'

'The Death Ride,' Pete said, leaping to his feet with surprising speed and agility. 'The route of the Death Ride goes dangerously close to the Perpetuity Chamber. I've managed to keep them away from the main vault that holds the Chamber, but the track does go very close. If the Drexxon has sabotaged the Death Ride . . . '

The Doctor jumped to his feet as well. 'It could crash through the vault wall,' he finished. 'But the Drexxon still has to open the Chamber itself. That must be sealed – tell me that's sealed.'

'It is secure,' Pete agreed. 'We locked it with something the Drexxons could never understand or manipulate, something that is the very opposite of the chaos and violence they live by.'

'Deadlock?' the Doctor asked. 'Double-bolt encryption? Stasis latch? What?'

Pete smiled. 'Much more powerful than that, Doctor. We sealed it with music.'

'Ah,' the Doctor said. 'Then I think we might have a problem.'

But before anyone could ask what he meant, or how a Chamber could be sealed with music, two small figures came running up.

'Harby and Vosh,' Amy exclaimed. 'What's the hurry?'

'You've got to come,' Harby gasped through his excitement. 'They've finished it.'

'Finished what?' the Doctor asked.

'The Death Ride,' Vosh said. 'If we're quick we can be on the first ride. People are queuing already. We thought you'd want to know.'

'Absolutely we want to know,' the Doctor

agreed. He grabbed Amy's hand and hauled her to her feet, repeating the action with Rory. 'If that Death Ride leaves the starting point, it will crash through into the secret vault and the Drexxon will open the Perpetuity Chamber.'

CHAPTER 11
STOP
THE
TRAIN

'Garvo is the key – literally,' the Doctor said, as they hurried back down the tunnels towards the Galactic Fair.

'I still don't get this music thing,' Rory admitted.

'As the Doctor says, the Drexxon must have had many "masters" like this over the years,' Perpetual Pete said. 'Ready for when it found the Chamber.' Pete hadn't been to the fair, so he had not seen Drexxon or Garvo. The Doctor and his friends had quickly explained the situation and what they'd found out.

'The Chamber is sealed with a musical key,'

the Doctor said. 'Literally a musical key. It's like a code, only instead of typing in numbers or letters, you play musical notes. Play the right notes or chords in the right sequence and it opens the Perpetuity Chamber.'

'But you still have to know the combination of notes, right?' Amy asked.

'Right. But think about it – Garvo has been seen wandering the tunnels playing his harmonica. Drexxon had to be sure that the Chamber was even here. He's probably been to hundreds of possible locations while travelling with the fair, or on his own. Now he knows, and he's been probing the defences, getting feedback in some way. Working out the combination so that – once he breaks into the vault – he knows how to open the Chamber. By now, he knows the exact musical notes to play.'

'I should have gone to the fair,' Perpetual Pete grumbled. 'If I had, I probably would have seen the Drexxon and I could have taken action to protect the Vault and the Chamber within it. But I thought it was a waste of time.'

'Having fun is never a waste of time, General,' the Doctor said.

Rory gasped. 'You mean he is – '

'Now I am just Pete,' the old man said, cutting off Rory's question.

'But Doctor,' Amy said, 'if Garvo is in a coma or whatever back at the fair, then how will Drexxon open the Chamber, even if the Death Ride does smash open the vault?'

The Doctor paused in mid-step. They were hurrying back along the main tunnel, and he hopped several times before coming to a halt.

'That's brilliant, Amy. Of course. We have to get to Garvo – without him, Drexxon's powerless.'

'He can still sabotage the Death Ride,' Rory pointed out.

'So – are we not going on the Death Ride,

then?' Harby asked.

'Absolutely not,' the Doctor told the two boys. 'It's dangerous.'

'Yes!' Vosh agreed. 'It's dangerous and wicked and cool.'

'No, no, no – not that sort of dangerous. I mean it's dangerous dangerous.'

The two boys looked at each other, obviously disappointed.

'Look,' the Doctor said, 'we need to get to the fair and make sure Garvo is all right and that Drexxon doesn't try to hurt him. I want you two – and Rory – to get to the Death Ride as quick as you can.'

'But not go on it?' Rory checked. 'Absolutely not to go on the dangerous up and down roller coaster ride thing, yes?'

'Yes. I mean, no – you don't go on it. You have to stop the Death Ride from operating. Make sure they don't try to run it. Do whatever you have to.'

Rory nodded. 'Leave it to us. Shouldn't be a problem.'

'Great,' the Doctor said. 'Off you go.'

Harby led Vosh and Rory down a side tunnel.

'Hey,' Perpetual Pete called after them, 'that tunnel's Off-Lim—' He stopped and shook his head. 'Oh, never mind,' he muttered.

The Galactic Fair was as crowded as ever. The Doctor, Amy and Perpetual Pete forced their way through the mass of people towards Garvo's tent.

'I can't see that I've missed much,' Pete said, as Clueless the Clown waved to them from his stilts. Pete glared back at him.

'Ever tried candyfloss?' Amy asked.

'Can't say that I have. What's special about candyfloss?'

'You know how usually with food, you eat it and then it's gone?' the Doctor said.

'Yes.'

'Well, with candyfloss – it's gone before you eat it!'

'Perfect food for time travellers,' Amy said.

'That and Backwards Bananas,' the Doctor agreed. 'Oh, and vomit fruit.'

'I don't want to know,' Amy insisted.

'The clever thing with that is,' the Doctor went on, ignoring her, 'it's so disgusting that just the thought of eating it makes you sick. And you're so sick you'll eat anything afterwards, even a vomit fruit. Effect and cause instead of the other way round. I try to avoid them myself,' he added, 'especially after that unfortunate incident with the Queen Mother.'

Finally they reached Garvo's tent. But when they hurried inside, the mattress on the floor was empty. Garvo had gone.

'Could he have just, I don't know, woken up and wandered off?' Amy asked.

The Doctor shook his head. 'Drexxon had to wake him by reconnecting the link. The leash has gone, and so has his harmonica.'

'But they'd have to be right there, inside the vault, to open the Perpetuity Chamber,' Pete said. 'And unless the vault is breached, they can't get inside.'

'They're heading for the Death Ride,' Amy realised. 'Drexxon will want to be on it when it crashes through the vault wall, if that's what's going to happen.'

'It is, unless Rory and his young friends can stop the ride,' the Doctor said.

'The Drexxon will do anything to prevent that,' Perpetual Pete told them. 'Your friend and the boys could be in great danger.'

'Death Ride?' Amy suggested.

The Doctor nodded. 'Death Ride.'

The start of the Death Ride was another

large cavern cut into the rock of the asteroid. The roof was so high it was out of sight. A tall scaffolding tower with steep steps built into the side of it stood in the centre of the cavern. People were already queuing all the way up the steps. The ride itself plunged down towards the floor, levelling out for about thirty metres, then dipping sharply down through a hole in the ground.

At the top of the ride, the Death Ride train was a string of eight small, green, open-topped compartments on wheels. It looked like a caterpillar about to climb down the curving stem of a leaf.

A large crowd of people had assembled to watch the first Death Ride. The Doctor, Amy and Perpetual Pete pushed and shoved their way through to the front.

'I just hope Rory is up there telling them not to let it go ahead,' the Doctor said.

'Guess again,' Amy told him. 'He's over there.'

Rory was standing with Harby and Vosh at the bottom of the steps. He saw the Doctor and Amy approaching and waved.

'Have you told them?' the Doctor demanded as soon as he was within earshot. 'Have you stopped the Death Ride?'

'Um,' Rory said. He looked at Harby and Vosh, who shuffled their feet in embarrassment. 'Sort of yes and no.'

'Meaning what?' Pete asked.

'Meaning, yes we've told them. And no, we haven't actually stopped it. Not as such. They're going ahead. In about five minutes, actually. Sorry about that.'

'Sorry?' the Doctor stared at him in astonishment. 'The Drexxons are about to be unleashed and everyone on that ride, to say nothing of all the other people on this asteroid, could die. Sorry?!'

'We did actually mention that,' Rory said sheepishly.

'Did you tell them what's going on?' Perpetual Pete asked.

Rory nodded. 'Yes. Yes, we did.'

Vosh explained: 'Rory was great. He told them that a nasty vicious alien space monkey had sabotaged the ride so it would crash and the alien space monkey could release its bloodthirsty, warlike race from a special prison that's been hidden for centuries and which can only be opened with a mouth organ.'

'They didn't seem to believe me,' Rory added.

'Possibly too much information, do you think?' the Doctor suggested. 'Maybe, "there's a slight technical problem with this ride, and everyone might die horribly in a crash," would have done?'

Rory nodded slowly. 'Possibly. You want to try?' he offered.

'Twenty!' someone yelled through a loudspeaker from the top of the tower. 'Nineteen!'

'I think it's a bit late for that.'

The crowd joined in the countdown.

'So, what now?' Amy asked. She had to shout to be heard above the countdown.

'Change of plan,' the Doctor decided. He looked at Rory through narrowed eyes. 'You and Amy . . . I'll talk to you two in a moment. First . . .' He crouched down to talk to Harby and Vosh. 'Can you find some of your friends from the orchestra? As many as you can, with their instruments. I need them here fast. In fact, faster than that!' He straightened up. 'How long do we have?' he asked Pete.

'It's a long ride. I guess that's part of the attraction. But I'd estimate it will pass closest to the vault in about eight minutes.'

'That's how long you have,' the Doctor told

the boys. 'Meet in the tunnel out there in less than eight minutes – the sooner, the better.' He pointed to the tunnel they'd come down. 'Now, scoot!'

The countdown reached zero. They all looked up at the rails, high above them, as with a rumble and roar, the Death Ride train started, ever so slowly, to move forwards.

'And what about us?' Amy asked.

The Death Ride was gathering speed, plunging down the track towards them.

'Anything we can do,' Rory shouted. 'Anything at all.'

The Doctor grinned. 'In which case, I want you on that train.'

'You are kidding!' Amy told him.

'Garvo and Drexxon are probably on board. You have to stop the ride safely, break the link between the two of them, and help anyone who gets hurt. OK?' He paused for less than a second

for any objections as the Death Ride hurtled
down the track. 'Well, off you go then.'

CHAPTER 12
DEATH RIDE

Catching the Train of Death, as Amy was already thinking of it, turned out to be easier than she expected. Or at least, not quite as difficult and dangerous. The train was already slowing as it reached the bottom of the scaffolding. The next section of track ran across the floor of the cavern before plunging sharply down through the ground to the level below.

But before it took the plunge, the train was designed to slow almost to a stop for a few moments. Partly, this was to heighten the excitement amongst the passengers. Partly, it was so that anyone who realised from the experience of the first, fairly tame, drop that they didn't actually want to continue with the ride could get off.

An automatic announcement warned people this really was their very last chance to get off the ride and to be careful leaving their carriage. Of course, no one was supposed to get on the ride at this stage. But Amy was already racing towards where the train had slowed right down. Rory was close behind her. The Doctor too was running, his floppy hair blown back out of his face for once. Perpetual Pete had made no effort to keep up with them and Amy could see him in the distance, shaking his head in sad disbelief.

The train was slowly starting to pick up speed again by the time they reached it.

'There are no spare seats,' Rory shouted.

'Wimp,' Amy shouted back.

The Doctor was leaning in over the side of the rear carriage, hurrying to keep up as the train started to pull away more quickly. He pointed at a young boy sitting with a couple of friends. 'You – are you in the orchestra?'

The boy looked round, then pointed to himself to ask: 'You mean me?'

'Yes, you,' the Doctor shouted. 'You are, aren't you? I saw you playing a trombone.'

The boy nodded guiltily, though he obviously had no idea what the problem was.

'Right,' the Doctor ordered, 'out!' Running to catch up with the next of the little green open-topped carriages, he caught sight of another child who was part of the orchestra – a small girl trying to hide behind a larger girl. 'And you – come on.'

'What's he doing?' Rory gasped.

The train was moving away faster now, heading for the hole in the floor of the cavern.

'Just get in,' Amy yelled at him, levering herself up and over the open side of the carriage. 'At least there are seats now,' she told Rory, as the Doctor lifted two more orchestra children bodily from the next carriage and dumped them on the ground beside him.

'Anyone else? Anyone else in the orchestra?' the Doctor shouted up the length of the train. 'If so, I want you off this train now. Understood? I'm not mucking about, this is important.'

A few hands slowly and nervously went up. A man, a young woman, two more boys and a girl undid their harnesses and climbed awkwardly off the train. They had to jump as the train picked up speed. Amy and Rory flopped down into spare seats next to each other.

'No time to sit down!' the Doctor shouted to them. 'You've got a job to do, remember?'

'And what about you and Pete?' Rory called back to him.

The train gathered speed, leaving the Doctor behind, with a small group of children and a couple of adults. His answer was almost lost in the rush of air and the screams of the people in the front carriage as it began to fall.

But Amy thought the Doctor called back: 'I'm hoping Pete has a skiffle board, and I'm going to organise a concert.'

But she didn't have time to worry about that. The train was picking up speed, leaving the Doctor and his new friends far behind. Amy stood up to see them disappear into the distance, but Rory pulled her back down again.

'But we need to look for Gravo and Drexxon,' Amy protested.

'Not just as we're about to start on the journey to the centre of Earth,' Rory told her.

As he finished speaking, screams of delight echoed from the carriage in front of them. The whole train was tipping and sliding into the hole in the ground. Moments later, their own carriage began to tip. Over the tops of the seats, Amy could see the whole length of the train — right to the small engine at the front. The engine that was plunging into the dark hole and dragging the other carriages with it.

The carriage continued to tip, until it seemed that Amy and everyone inside would fall out of it. Then they were hurtling down into the blackness, and Amy was screaming as loudly as anyone. Except possibly Rory, whose shrieks were so loud they hurt Amy's ears.

'Geronimo!' Amy yelled, as the darkness closed over her.

'That's my line,' the Doctor complained as Amy's cry — accompanied by shrieks and wails and screams — floated back to where he was standing.

'So what do you want us to do then, Mister?' one of the boys the Doctor had just pulled off the train asked.

'It's "Doctor", all right? Don't ever forget that. Doc-tor,' he pronounced it carefully and precisely.

'So, what do you want us to do then, Mister Doc-tor?' another of the boys asked. A girl clicked her tongue and shook her head.

'We are going to give a concert,' the Doctor said. 'You are going to find as many of your friends in the orchestra as you can in the next five minutes.' He looked round at the crowds. Already people were queuing for the next ride. 'Then we meet out there in the tunnel.'

'What if we don't have our instruments?' the clicky-tongue girl asked.

'Then you hum and sing and clap your hands.'

'Do you play an instrument?' one of the grown-ups asked. Their tone suggested they thought he didn't.

'Only if you count the spoons, and I didn't bring any. No,' the Doctor said proudly, his chest swelling, 'I shall be your conductor. Now, hurry up. I've got Harby and Vosh looking for people too, so with luck we'll have enough. See you in four and a half minutes, right?'

'Right,' they all agreed.

None of them really had any idea what was going on, but it sounded like it might be fun.

Perpetual Pete was the one person who didn't have a smile on his face. But then, the Doctor thought, his face wasn't really built for smiling. 'You think this'll work?' he asked the Doctor.

'Oh, yes. Probably. I'll need to know the exact run of musical notes to open the Chamber, though,' the Doctor told him.

'If I can remember what it is. It's been a while. But we can't open the Chamber – that's the last thing we want to do.'

'I agree,' the Doctor said. 'But I still need to know the right chords to do it.'

Several levels below where the Doctor and Perpetual Pete were standing, and travelling much, much faster, the Death Ride took another plunge. This one was quite tame compared with that first dive into the ground. But it still left Amy feeling that her stomach was floating somewhere back down the track and she would probably never see it again.

'Time to make our move, I guess,' Rory said, getting carefully to his feet as the ride levelled out again.

'How do you suggest we get to the other carriages and the engine?' Amy asked.

Rory looked at her and she saw how pale he had grown. 'I think we have to climb across.'

'While the train's going?'

Rory nodded.

'At about a hundred miles an hour?'

Rory swallowed and nodded again.

'With the Train of Death liable to drop into the ground or fly up into the air at any moment while we're doing it?'

'Problem?' Rory asked. His voice seemed to

have risen in pitch.

'No,' Amy told him. 'No problem at all. Let's get started.'

She grabbed Rory's arm for support as the train lurched and dived again.

CHAPTER 13
FINE TUNING

Despite understanding better than anyone the threat they faced, Perpetual Pete was beginning to enjoy himself. In the early years, when the miners first arrived, it had been a challenge to keep the digging and tunnelling away from the Perpetuity Chamber hidden in its Vault deep inside the asteroid. Not that the challenge was anything like as great as commanding the Combined Stellar Forces armies in their war against the Drexxons . . . But that was when Perpetual Pete was a much younger man.

Gradually, the miners had come to accept Pete, if not actually to respect him as much as he'd have liked. They grew used to his constant arguments about health and safety. They believed he was acting in their best interests — which of course he was. Just not quite in the way they imagined.

But then, they imagined he was being paid by the Mining Conglomerates and had some official status. It was all bluff. IMC and the others had no idea that Pete even existed. If they had thought he was making the mining for trisilicate and duralinium harder and more expensive than it needed to be, they'd have been very angry indeed.

It had been a difficult job calling for tact and diplomacy as much as stubbornness and determination. But over the years it had got easier and now everyone took what Pete said for granted. If he told them a tunnel was Off-Limits, they accepted that. Since they had the whole of the rest of the asteroid to mine, keeping them away from one small area had not actually been too much of a problem.

Until now.

The Death Ride needed to be kept away from the working mine areas. No one wanted it to interfere with the mining, and everyone understood the possible hazards of having a fairground ride set up where robot equipment was used to having the place to itself as it tunnelled and mined, detonated explosives to expose new ore seams and routinely pumped out the air from areas where there might be a gas pocket so as to avoid explosions.

It was almost inevitable that the Galactic Fair would want to run their Death Ride through some of the Off-Limits areas. Pete had managed to steer them away from the tunnels that went nearest to the vault. But even so, the tracks were closer than he'd have liked in a couple of areas.

He had the route marked on a plan in his

pocket, which he now showed the Doctor. Pete smoothed out the stained paper, and jabbed a wrinkled finger at where the vault was located. Of course, it wasn't actually marked. But Pete had drawn a blue line to show the route of the Death Ride.

'I think the most likely point of sabotage would be here.' He indicated a place where the blue line turned sharply away from the vault area.

The Doctor nodded. 'If the Drexxon derails the Death Ride, it will carry on through the tunnel wall and breach the vault. That's at the bottom of a huge drop, so it'll be going very fast indeed.'

'I'll get in touch with Korl and get him to send whatever emergency equipment he can to that section,' Pete said. 'Could be a lot of casualties though,' he added quietly.

'I know. And Amy and Rory are riding on that thing.'

It was a nightmare. Amy and Rory had agreed that Rory would try to get to the engine. Amy agreed that he might have a better idea of how to stop the ride than she did. Amy's job was to find Drexxon and Garvo and break the link between them.

Rory wasn't happy about that. Drexxon was likely to attack Amy as soon as he saw her. But Amy reckoned that she could get help from other passengers. And once Garvo had recovered from the shock, he would surely help too.

'Anyway, he might not even be on board,' she pointed out. She had to shout over the sound of the wheels on the track and the wind rushing past.

'I still think we should stay together.'

Amy shook her head. 'You get to the engine as quick as you can and stop this thing.' She didn't like to have to admit it, but Rory would be quicker than her working his way along the train and leaping from carriage to carriage. She would keep up as best she could, but once she saw Garvo and Drexxon she'd deal with them, while Rory still needed to stop the train.

'Health and Safety. Just doing an in-ride assessment,' Rory told the startled passengers in the next carriage as he landed with a bump on the pitching floor.

Amy leaped after him – just as the train dropped away down another steep slope. Rory leaned back and grabbed her hands, dragging her into the carriage after him.

Getting to the next carriage was even more dangerous. Rory jumped just as the train veered round a bend. Amy watched helplessly as he leaped out into space, the train twisting away beneath him. But, somehow, Rory managed to flail his arms and scrabble at the side of the carriage as he fell. The train lurched back the other way and Rory was hurled up in the air, to land with a painful-sounding bump in the back of the carriage.

'All part of the show,' he gasped, waving away helping hands. 'I'll be collecting tips later.'

Amy was careful to time her own jump on a flat, straight section. But that meant she had to wait, and she could see Rory using the same section to make his own leap into the next carriage along. He turned to wave back at Amy.

'Keep going!' she yelled.

Rory frowned, cupping his hand round his ear to show he hadn't heard what she said.

Amy shook her head and pointed forwards. 'Keep going,' she mouthed.

Rory's frown deepened as he worked it out. Then he smiled and gave her a thumbs up. Just as the train roared sharply upwards, knocking Rory off his feet. Amy also stumbled, and found herself sitting on the lap of a rather surprised elderly man.

'Um, refreshments?' Amy said.

'Ice cream?'

'Sorry, all out of ice cream. And hot drinks aren't really recommended,' she added as the train turned again and she was thrown across the carriage. Children and adults alike whooped with delight.

There were about twenty people assembled in the tunnel with the Doctor and Perpetual Pete. About half of those had instruments. The Doctor got Harby and Vosh to organise them into sections according to what instrument they had or usually played.

'If you don't have your instrument with you, just make the noise. So if you play the trumpet, it's . . . ' He did his best to make a trumpet noise.

Then he demonstrated drums, flute and finally bagpipes. The bagpipes earned him a small round of applause.

Right, now, off we go. Drum Major Pete will lead the way – boom-boom-boom, remember, Pete.'

Pete raised a wispy eyebrow and didn't answer.

'Where are we going?' Harby asked as Perpetual Pete marched quickly down the tunnel and everyone hurried after him.

'As close as we can get to a secret Perpetuity Chamber concealed inside a hidden vault. I'm hoping our music will echo along the tunnel and the programme of music I've prepared will prevent that vault from opening. That clear enough for you?'

Everyone shook their heads and told him, 'No.'

'Good.' The Doctor extended his sonic screwdriver, raising it like a conductor's baton. 'Right then, we start with *When the Saints Go Marching In*, I hope you know that one. Play it loud and play it with passion. Play it like your lives depend on it. Because . . .' The Doctor tapped his makeshift baton on an imaginary music stand. ' . . . because they do.'

CHAPTER 14
INTO THE VAULT

'There is just a chance,' Amy yelled to anyone who would listen, 'that we are going to crash. So hold on tight.'

'Crash?' a small boy nearby echoed. 'Terrific!'

'No, actually,' Amy told him. 'Not terrific. Not even remotely terrific. This isn't part of the ride, it's a proper, real, serious warning, all right?'

'All right,' the boy said sulkily.

'So hold on, then,' Amy told him. 'And you,' she told his friends.

She had lost sight of Rory, and she still had not seen Drexxon and Garvo. What if they weren't on board at all? What if the train wasn't going to crash? How embarrassing would that be? 'Come on, Pond,' she muttered to herself. Never mind being embarrassed. If the ride didn't crash that would be a good thing – a terrific thing.

She timed her jump carefully, and leaped into the next carriage. As she jumped, she could see Rory, about three carriages ahead, waving and pointing.

'Excuse me. Health and safety. Hold on tight in case we crash. But first, budge up a bit,' Amy told a woman clutching the arm of a man on the back seat of the carriage. She'd landed just in front of them and now she shoved them aside enough to climb up on the seat.

'Careful,' the man warned, trying to push her down again. 'That's not safe.'

But Amy shook off his attentions. She could see Rory, still pointing, and gave him a thumbs up. He glared back at her like she was mad, and pointed again, jabbing his finger urgently.

A moment later he disappeared in a blur of brown fur as the Drexxon leaped at him.

'Give me strength,' Amy said and ran for the front of the carriage. The ride dipped and turned, throwing her sideways.

'Coming through!' she yelled as she kept going, hurling herself into the next carriage. She could see Rory now, just one carriage ahead. Drexxon was tearing at him. Garvo was pushing away anyone who tried to help Rory.

Amy sprinted, suddenly running uphill as the ride rose steeply. Any moment it would plunge down again. She ran and jumped, just as the train dipped, and found herself falling towards the next carriage. She slammed into Garvo, sending him flying.

But the leash remained attached to the Drexxon, who was still battering relentlessly at Rory.

'Get off my Rory!' Amy yelled at the Drexxon.

She grabbed the furry creature round the middle and wrenched him away. Immediately the Drexxon turned its attack on Amy. Rory staggered to his feet – falling down again as the ride lurched round a steep bend.

'Never mind me – get to the engine,' Amy shouted. 'Stop this thing before it crashes!'

'Crashes?' a young man sitting nearby repeated.

'Yes. We're going to crash. So hold on tight. Brace yourselves,' Amy shouted back, still wrestling with the Drexxon. 'Pass it on. Tell the person next to you, and pass it on along the carriages.'

Garvo was getting to his feet. But Rory shoved him out of the way as he hurried past, heading for the next carriage. The engine was only a few carriages away now. Amy just hoped Rory would get to it in time. And that he'd be able to do something when he did.

But she didn't have much time to worry about Rory, because the Drexxon was clutching at her face, scratching her hands as she tried to hold the creature off, nipping and biting at her with its sharp teeth . . .

'Well, help me!' she gasped at the nearest person, the young man she'd just spoken to.

'You told me to hold on tight,' he said. 'Make your mind up.'

'Help me first,' Amy said through gritted teeth and a face full of attacking fur. 'Then hold on tight.'

Rory too was shouting warnings as he raced through the last couple of carriages. He could see the front of the train – heading right for a rock wall. Rory threw his hands up in front of his face and dived to the floor. At the last moment, the Death Ride swerved violently sideways. The rock wall shot past, and the train dived down again, bouncing Rory painfully across the floor.

'You part of the act, sonny?' a grizzled old miner with a straggly grey beard asked.

'Better believe it,' Rory told him. 'Hold on tight, old timer – this thing could crash at any moment.'

'Runaway mine train, you reckon?' the old man asked. 'Wouldn't be the first,' he added knowingly.

Rory pulled himself to his feet and staggered to the front of the little carriage. Just one more jump, he told himself – one more, then all he had to do was tell the driver to put the brakes on and stop the train.

Rory got up speed as the train dived downwards, and took a running jump out of the end of the carriage. The old miner and several other people applauded.

He slammed painfully to the floor of the front carriage. It was smaller than the others. The engine. In front of him Rory could see a panel with lots of levers, switches and knobs. There were several dials and read-outs on it too. One seemed to be the speed, another showed direction of travel, a third was timing the ride. Rory briefly surveyed the switches and levers – one of which must be the brake. The driver would know.

But as Rory looked round desperately for the driver, he realised he was alone in the carriage. There was no driver. It was all automated. There was no one there who could stop the Death Ride.

No one except Rory.

He didn't waste time worrying. There was no time left to waste. Instead, Rory pulled the nearest lever – and the train increased speed. He shoved the lever back into place, but the speed didn't reduce. So Rory pressed buttons and turned knobs and pulled other levers.

It made no difference. The train was hurtling ever faster through the rocky tunnels, and at any moment Rory knew it might reach the section of track that the Drexxon had sabotaged.

'What would the Doctor do?' Rory wondered out loud. He didn't have a sonic screwdriver, so the obvious answer was no use.

But another thought occurred to Rory. 'What would the Doctor do if he didn't have his sonic screwdriver?' He pulled off his shoe and hammered at the controls with it.

Sparks erupted from the control panel. A small explosion blew off an access panel and Rory reached inside to grab handfuls of smoking wires and rip them free. He felt a jolt of electricity up his arm, like someone had thumped the funny bone in his elbow.

But, miraculously, the train did seem to be slowing. Rory breathed a long, heartfelt sigh of relief.

Then he realised the train was slowing because it was going steeply uphill. It almost stopped, teetering on the brink of the deepest, darkest, sharpest, most terrifying drop yet.

'Hang on!' came Amy's voice from somewhere behind Rory. It was advice he didn't need. He grabbed hold of the side of the little carriage as the Death Ride plunged down again, faster than ever, gathering speed. Heading straight for a rock wall.

Rory could see that the track was designed to veer sharply away from the rock wall at the last moment. He could also see that there was a short section of track missing. This was the place. This was the sabotage. Desperately he grabbed more wires and cables and pulled them free, holding on tight with his other hand.

More sparks, more explosions. A screech of brakes, and the train began to slow. He must have triggered some emergency system, Rory realised.

But there was no time to celebrate. The sudden slowing of the train was throwing people to the floor. Rory could hear shouts and warnings from the carriages. And he could see that although it was slowing down, the train was still going to leave the rails and hammer into the tunnel wall.

A few moments earlier, with the help of the other passengers, Amy had finally managed to hurl the Drexxon away from her and across the small carriage.

The train was plunging downwards, gathering speed.

'Hang on!' Amy yelled as loud as she could. Somehow she felt this was the moment — maybe it was instinct, or maybe it was the way the Drexxon was laughing as it scampered back to Garvo.

The two of them — human and alien monkey creature — grabbed hold of the safety rail across the front of one of the seats.

At the same moment, there was an ear-piercing scream. Amy looked round at the other passengers, but the noise seemed to be coming from outside the train. From under the train.

'Sounds like the brakes,' someone yelled above the shrieking.

People were thrown across the carriage, though Garvo and Drexxon were still clinging on tight to their rail. Sparks were spraying from the wheels, raining out and down from the Death Ride like a sparkler on firework's night.

Amy found she was laughing. 'Oh, Rory – you're a genius. Rory, I love you!' she shouted.

But her words were lost in the sound of the brakes and the roar of shattering metal as the train left the broken tracks and smashed headlong into the tunnel wall. Rocks and boulders crashed down on to the Death Ride train. Dust and debris whipped past Amy's face. It seemed as if the whole tunnel was collapsing as people went flying.

Then suddenly everything was silent. Cautiously looking up, Amy saw that the Death Ride train was stuck half through the tunnel wall. The engine was out of sight – hanging down into the darkness on the other side of the wall the train had smashed through. Into the vault that Perpetual Pete had hidden and protected for so long.

The train creaked as the weight of the engine dragged it slowly forwards, into the darkness.

'Rory!' Amy yelled.

But there was no answer.

CHAPTER 15
MUSICAL KEY

The train was rocking gently back and forth, creaking. Slowly, it inched forwards, into the black hole in the tunnel wall as the weight of the engine dragged the other carriages along the broken tracks.

Amy's thoughts were on Rory. But as the people around her picked themselves up and she saw the tear-stained, frightened faces of several children, she realised she had a greater priority.

'We have to get off this thing,' she said. 'It could slip forwards and into that hole at any moment.'

'If the scaffolding underneath us doesn't

collapse first,' someone added.

As soon as he spoke, there was a worrying creak from below, followed by a clatter of falling metal. Then the back of the carriage dropped abruptly by several metres.

Then there was another sound. A sad music that hung in the air.

'No!' Amy yelled.

In her worry about Rory and the other passengers on the Death Ride she had forgotten about Garvo and Drexxon. Garvo had the mouth organ to his lips and was playing what had to be the opening code for the Perpetuity Chamber.

Amy hurled herself across the carriage, desperate to knock the harmonica from Garvo's grasp. But the Drexxon leaped towards her, claws out and teeth bared. Its small furry face was twisted into a mask of triumph.

The haunting melody continued to fill the air.

Amy managed to stop herself. The Drexxon was inches from her face, the leash attaching it to Garvo's wrist was tight, so it couldn't get any closer to Amy. But equally, Amy couldn't get to Garvo. She couldn't stop him from playing the opening code.

There was another sound now – a wrenching, scraping of metal. But it wasn't coming from the train or the scaffolding. It was coming from inside the dark hole in the tunnel wall. Light flickered inside, throwing monstrous shadows on to the walls of the tunnel nearby.

The Perpetuity Chamber was opening.

When the Death Ride smashed through the tunnel wall – and breached the hidden vault – Rory was thrown forwards. He found himself lying on the control panel he had been desperately working at. Sparks erupted from it all around him. Somehow the panel had become the floor.

It took him a while to work out that the engine was hanging down through the hole in the tunnel wall. Above him he could see the first carriage teetering on the brink. Flickering light illuminated the broken metal edge of what must be the vault.

But the light wasn't coming from the sparks, or even the slight glow of the tunnel walls outside the vault.

As his ears recovered from the tremendous noise of the crash, Rory realised he could hear something else. A wrenching, scraping of metal was coming from below him. The whole engine was swinging slightly. The tiniest movement could send it falling. Gently and carefully, Rory twisted so he could peer cautiously over the edge of the panel and down into the darkness.

Except, it wasn't darkness. There was light down there – a flickering light that shone through a crack in the ground. As Rory watched, the crack began to widen. It was slowly pulling apart. From somewhere above he could now just make out the haunting sound of music – of Garvo's harmonica.

And in response, the ground was splitting open.

The Perpetuity Chamber was opening.

Rory pulled back, afraid of what he might see. The engine rocked and trembled ominously beneath him, slipping a few centimetres towards the ground. Somehow, Rory managed to stand up. Reaching above his head, and standing on tiptoe, he still couldn't reach the ragged edge of the broken tunnel wall. There was only one thing for it – he would have to climb up the engine, and into the carriage above.

But could he do that without falling? Could he do it without his weight dragging the carriage after the engine into the Vault as well? He could see dark shapes looking down at him now – was

one of them Amy? He hardly dared hope she
was all right.

The thought she might be hurt, that there
would be people injured who he could help if
only he could get to them, spurred Rory into
action. He grabbed hold of the twisted side of
the engine and hauled himself up. Bit by bit he
managed to climb up towards the ragged hole
above. Almost there . . .

He reached out and grabbed the rough edge
of the hole in the tunnel with one hand. Then
the other. He pushed off with his toes, trying to
get a better grip – and found himself swinging
from the rock. He could feel it crumbling under
his hands as he desperately pulled himself up.
If he fell now, he would plunge down into the
Perpetuity Chamber below.

Despite himself, despite knowing he didn't
want to see, Rory looked down into the growing
light. What he saw almost made him lose his grip

entirely. Then he redoubled his efforts to climb up and out, breathing heavily, straining every muscle, fighting to keep his panic under control.

The ground had split wide open. Brilliant white light was pouring out of the open Chamber. And out of the light came darkness. Black shapes were hauling themselves up and out of the ground, just as Rory was trying to escape through the opening into the tunnel above him.

Massive paws with claws the size of large tent pegs slashed at the sides of the tunnel as the enormous creatures emerged. Their dark matted fur glistened with oily slime. Teeth like tombstones snapped together hungrily. The Drexxons were coming . . .

The Doctor's hand froze in mid air as he conducted. He was walking backwards down the tunnels, glancing over his shoulder to check he wasn't going to walk into the wall or anything daft as he followed Perpetual Pete. The sound of the crash echoed down the tunnels. For a moment, the entire orchestra stopped playing.

'Not good,' the Doctor said as the noise died away.

'The automated mining equipment should be there any moment if it hasn't already arrived,' Perpetual Pete said. 'It's trained for rescue and recovery.'

The faintest sound of a harmonica lingered in the air before the Doctor said: 'Is it trained to hold off an angry horde of Drexxons?'

Pete shook his head grimly. 'You'll need an army for that.'

'Or a do-it-yourself orchestra,' the Doctor said. He raised his sonic screwdriver baton again. 'Right, everyone – once more, from the top, with feeling.'

Amy reached down to grab Rory's shoulders, and with the help of a couple of other passengers heaved him into the carriage. He tumbled forwards and lay gasping for a moment. Then he leaped to his feet.

'Those things are coming. They've got out,' he said urgently.

'I couldn't stop Garvo playing the music code,' Amy admitted.

Behind them, the small Drexxon snapped its teeth and clicked its claws, raking them through the air in triumph.

'Yeah,' Rory said. 'See what you mean. And it's too late now. We have to get out of this thing. Anyone hurt?'

Red flashing lights shone up from the tunnel below. Looking down, Amy could see vehicles manoeuvring into position. A ladder extended from the top of one of them, thrusting up towards the Death Ride.

'Help's arrived,' she said.

But Rory was watching the Drexxon and

Garvo hurrying to the hole in the tunnel.

'They're getting away!' Amy realised as the small creature leaped through the hole.

'Let them,' Rory told her. 'What can they do?'

Almost immediately, they found out. The throbbing of the train's engine started up again. The whole Death Ride lurched forwards, towards the hole.

'They've started the engine. They're dragging us in!' Amy said.

'The engine must power the wheels of all the carriages,' Rory realised.

'What is it with boys and trains? Not interested,' Amy told him. 'Only interested in getting everyone off this ride. OK?'

'OK.'

The train was a twisted wreck, wheels snagged on the rails, carriages torn and damaged. But the engine was so powerful that it was dragging the wreckage slowly but surely towards the hole. The front carriage was lurching forwards, tipping into the void.

Amy and Rory helped everyone climb back into the next carriage. The ladders from the robot mining equipment could reach the carriages further back that had fallen lower as the scaffolding collapsed. It was still supporting them, just. But the whole structure was creaking and bending.

Luckily, most of the injuries seemed to be just cuts and bruises. Many of the passengers were in shock. But getting them off the ride was the first priority. Rory managed to make a sling for a boy with a broken arm, using someone else's coat. A woman who couldn't move her leg or feel her toes had to be carried by two of the stronger men . . .

The train continued to lurch slowly forwards, making the evacuation difficult and hazardous. But finally Amy and Rory were the last two people to climb down the ladder.

'We made it,' Rory said, laughing with relief. 'We all made it.'

Amy stopped a few rungs above him, suddenly overcome by a terrible realisation.

Rory could see it in her expression as she looked down at him. 'What is it?'

'We didn't all make it,' Amy said. 'Garvo's still there. He's still attached to Drexxon, still under the creature's control.'

'So, what can we do?'

Amy came to a decision. 'I'm going back for him,' she said. And she started back up the ladder to the Death Ride train as it lurched forwards again – towards the drop into the Perpetuity Chamber and the vicious Drexxons clambering out of it.

CHAPTER 16
THE AWAKENING

Various automated vehicles were already in position around the damaged scaffolding. Ladders had extended upwards and allowed the passengers to climb down. The whole structure creaked and groaned, and the Death Ride train lurched forwards towards the hole torn in the tunnel wall.

'Are we too late?' Perpetual Pete wondered.

Light was spilling out from the hole in the tunnel wall – blindingly white light. Silhouetted against the light was a tiny figure.

'That's Amy,' the Doctor realised, as the figure disappeared through the hole in the wall.

'What's she doing?'

Pete was shielding his eyes from the glare. 'Your friend Rory, too,' he pointed out.

Another dark figure, tiny at this distance, was clambering along the wreckage of the train.

'The Perpetuity Chamber is already open,' the Doctor said. 'We can't allow any of the Drexxons out before we close it up again. But we can stop it opening any further.'

'I'll get your friends out of there and see if it's safe to close the chamber,' Pete said.

The Doctor thanked him, and turned back to his orchestra. 'Right – slight change of plan. *Jerusalem*!'

'There's no need for language, Doctor,' Pete told him sternly. 'Especially in front of the children.'

'No no no – I want the orchestra to play the music *Jerusalem*.'

But Pete had already gone, hurrying towards

one of the robot mining machines that had a flat metal platform attached to the end of a long, flexible, jointed arm.

Amy lowered herself down through the hole in the tunnel wall and towards the bright light. She could see vague shapes in the brilliance – dark smudges that were rising up towards her. Indistinct, but terrifying. She could hear the hungry snarls and roars of the fully grown Drexxons as they climbed out of the Perpetuity Chamber and sensed freedom after their centuries of imprisonment.

Her eyes slowly adjusted to the bright light, and she could make out the shapes of Garvo and the small, original Drexxon. Everything was tilted and moving. The engine was hanging down into the vault. As Amy tried to climb down, the whole of the front carriage she was on shifted, and fell. It plummeted for several stomach-churning seconds before jolting to a stop.

Amy was thrown forwards, down into the engine. She slammed into the control panel, which was now, in effect, the floor. Sparks shot past her and the whole train rocked forwards again. Painfully, she pulled herself to her feet, feeling the entire train tremble with her every movement.

She had barely got her balance when Garvo appeared in front of Amy.

'You're too late,' he hissed. 'The vault has been breached and the Chamber is open!'

'So why are you still trying to move the train?' Amy demanded, ducking out of the way of the blow that Garvo aimed at her.

'The Drexxons are free! After countless years, they are free again. And they are hungry!'

Amy sidestepped another swipe. The small Drexxon was also grabbing for her. There wasn't much room to get away from them in the cramped, upended engine.

'So, what do Drexxons eat?' Even as she

asked the question, Amy was afraid she could guess the answer. She was right.

'People!' Garvo said.

'Well, that's a shame, because me and Rory got everyone off the ride. So I guess they'll only eat you.'

Garvo's hand whipped out and grabbed Amy's shoulder, clutching it painfully tight. 'And you,' he said.

Close beside him, the Drexxon snickered with amusement.

'Not if I can help it,' Amy gasped.

Although Garvo was holding her tight, that also meant that Amy could reach the leash that ran from his wrist to the Drexxon. Ignoring the pain in her shoulder, she grabbed the leash and wrenched it as hard as she could. The leash snapped with a crack like a gunshot.

Immediately, Garvo's grip loosened and, with a wail, he sank to his knees, supporting himself by still holding less tightly to Amy's shoulder.

She grabbed him under the arm. 'Come on – let's get you out of here.'

But Garvo was a dead weight. He seemed to have fainted. And there was no way Amy could carry him, let alone climb out of the engine, across the next carriage and up through the hole in the tunnel to safety.

The bright light seemed to dim as the dark mass of a huge Drexxon reached the level of the engine as it clawed and climbed its way up out of the Perpetuity Chamber. A massive paw reached out towards Amy and Garvo.

Rory stumbled back towards the hole in the tunnel wall. The light was getting brighter. But huge shadows were cast across the rock face – the shadows of the approaching Drexxons.

'Amy – come back!' he yelled. But his words were lost in the screech of protesting metal as the Death Ride train slid forwards again. 'Or at least wait for me,' he muttered, as he tried to keep his balance.

'Need any help there, young fella?'

Rory stumbled to a halt in astonishment. Perpetual Pete was standing beside the carriage. Not in it, but beside it.

'Only, you look like you need help to me.'

Rory just stared. Pete was standing in what ought to be mid air. 'How are you doing that?'

Perpetual Pete laughed. Somewhere in the middle, he burped loudly. 'Step aboard and find out. But make it quick – we need to rescue Amy.'

Amy threw herself backwards, dragging Garvo's unconscious body with her. The massive Drexxon paw slashed through the empty air where they had just been.

'You having fun?' Rory asked.

Amy stared up at him. He seemed to be

standing in mid air, beside the engine.

'Don't just lie there gawping,' Perpetual Pete said. He was standing next to Rory, holding what looked like a TV remote control.

'Let me help.' Rory jumped into the engine and hoisted Garvo over his shoulders. 'Come on.'

When Amy stood up, she could see that there was a metal platform beside the engine. It was attached to a flexible metal arm that extended down through the hole in the tunnel wall above them, pivoted so that the platform remained level and upright.

'Make it quick,' Pete warned.

The nearest Drexxon had pulled its paw back ready for another strike. It swung at the platform. But Pete worked a control on the remote, and the platform lifted quickly out of the way.

Amy had almost forgotten about the small Drexxon that had controlled Garvo. But now it launched itself at her and Rory, in a rage. At the same time, the enormous Drexxon that had climbed level with the train grabbed hold of the engine and hauled itself across.

'Jump!' Rory yelled. He leaped, with Garvo across his shoulders, to the platform.

Amy followed. She landed close to Rory, and saw that Garvo's eyes were open and he was staring at her in surprise and fear.

'Don't worry,' she told him. 'We'll soon be out of here. Won't we?' she asked Pete.

He smiled, and worked the remote. The platform rose rapidly, neatly dodging another attempted blow from the huge Drexxon.

Below her, Amy could see more of the enormous creatures climbing up towards them. The platform continued to rise, the arm twisting so the platform remained level and the right way up as it withdrew through the hole.

There was little clearance. And as they were drawn back through the tunnel wall, the whole of the Death Ride train gave a final lurch under the weight of the huge Drexxon that was now clinging to the engine.

Amy caught a confused glimpse of the small Drexxon snarling angrily at the huge one, as if telling it off. Then the train fell – taking both creatures with it. It plunged down towards the bright light, crashing into the other emerging creatures as it fell, and taking them back down with it. For a moment, the shadows and silhouettes blotted out the bright light. Then they were gone.

'Now!' Pete yelled over the side of the platform. 'Now, Doctor! They're all back inside – close the Perpetuity Chamber.'

Far below, the Doctor wielded his sonic screwdriver and took the orchestra into its next piece of music. It was one of his favourites, and he sang along with the music as it echoed round the tunnels.

'Klokleda partha mennin klatch . . . '

The fact that it was a lullaby seemed very appropriate.

CHAPTER 17
ENCORE

With the train gone, plummeting into the depths of the hidden vault, Perpetual Pete kept the observation platform on its long metal arm positioned close to the hole in the tunnel wall.

The light was fading as the Perpetuity Chamber slowly closed. The massive shaggy form of a Drexxon tried to squeeze between the closing sides, but was forced back. For a moment, its huge, savage paw stuck out of the ground, before the light faded and the paw was swallowed up. It sank back into the Perpetuity Chamber like the last struggle of a drowning man . . .

Slowly, gently, the metal arm retracted and the platform lowered to the ground. Amy was clutching Rory in a hug. Garvo was waking up, and looking round in confusion. Perpetual Pete was grinning, his white beard twitching as he laughed.

'Are you all right?' Amy asked Garvo.

He nodded. 'I think so. It's all a bit muzzy to be honest. But . . . ' He looked round anxiously.

'Yes?' Rory prompted.

'What is that awful smell?'

Perpetual Pete's grin faded back into his beard. 'Let's not get personal, sunshine.'

Amy ran to the Doctor, who was still conducting furiously. The music swelled and rose to its climax.

'It's all right,' Amy told him. 'The Perpetuity Chamber is closed – you did it. You can stop now.'

The Doctor's face was fixed in concentration. 'No, I can't,' he said.

'Why – what's wrong?'

'What's wrong? Are you mad?' The Doctor spread his hands, to slow the music to a close. Then he turned to Amy. 'We can't stop now,' he told her. 'We haven't done *Land of Hope and Glory* yet. And what's more . . . ' he grinned hugely. 'I'm having such fun. Right everyone, you'll need to know the words of the chorus.'

Before long the whole tunnel was full of people. Some were heroic survivors of the Death Ride. Others had been drawn to this tunnel by the sound of the orchestra. All were clapping their hands, playing instruments (or making the sounds of them), and joining in the chorus. Harby and Vosh played like they had never played before, grinning from ear to ear and yelling out the words they had just learned. Perpetual Pete tapped his feet in something close to the correct rhythm.

'Here we go again,' Rory yelled in delight.

'*Land of Hope and Glory . . .*'

'You're mad,' Amy told him delightedly. 'We're all mad.'

Garvo shook his head. 'I don't know what's going on,' he said. 'But it's amazing.'

'Oh – nearly forgot,' Rory told him. 'I picked this up.' He pulled something from his pocket and handed it to Garvo. It was his harmonica.

'Solo spot!' the Doctor yelled, pointing his baton-sonic screwdriver at Garvo. 'Whatever you like. Just make it up as you go along.'

'Make it up?' Amy said. 'He's just faced the most terrible danger, been captured and hypnotised by an alien space monkey and you want him to make it up as he goes along?'

'Works for me,' the Doctor told her. 'A one, a two, a one, two, three and – cue Garvo!'

The crowd listened in silence to the harmonica music. A haunting, lilting melody.

Music that made them both happy and sad at the same time. Sounds that affected their emotions and played with their feelings in the way that only music can.

The End